Written Off

Written Off

The Invisible, Book 1

BY
CATHERINE A. LAMPSHIRE

ISBN: 978-1-7352127-4-6 (Print)

ISBN: 978-1-7352127-5-3 (E-book)

DEDICATION

Doug, you have loved me regardless of my shape and size. I am more than a number on a scale and cloths size. With your love, support, and encouragement I can truly be myself and learn to accept and love who I am. At least that is one thing the HOA can't take away!

The truth will set you free, but first it will piss you off.

—Gloria Steinem

PROLOGUE

"Sam, is that your back deck motion sensor going off?" Keevan asks, gesturing his thumb toward the patio door. "The thing keeps flickering."

"Is someone at the back door?" Foster asks in alarm, cramming the book we've been discussing deep into the seat cushion.

I have to bite back a chuckle. Then swallow a bit nervously. Yeah, guy's got a point.

A bunch of my buddies, mostly motorcycle biking bros, are currently here at my home. We've been discussing our latest read. A work of fiction…Okay, it's a romance novel. Written by one of our favorite newer authors, Sonsy Falstaff.

The guys and I got turned onto Falstaff—and onto reading books—by initially independently reading some of her stuff. When we manned up and realized that most of us had actually read one, the same one we'd been passing around, we began earnestly discussing it. That led from one thing to another until this. A book club. Males only. Secret.

"Lighten up, Bro. Just pretend you don't see or hear anything," I tell him, including the others.

Don't want to spook her. Don't want her to think that I'm onto her. Though my words sound calm, in reality, I'm quivering with excitement. Nerves and muscles drawn taut, ready to spring up to take a peek and see for myself.

"Why didn't the light work like it's supposed to?" asks Joe, my business partner in security systems. Half rising from his seat, he cranes his neck to have a look.

"I loosened the bulb so it only flickers a few times before going dark."

That earns me an are-you-fucking-crazy look. Then it dawns on him. "Food fairy?" he asks. Eager hopefulness has him tiptoe-prancing to the window to check. Others follow suit.

Joe, the Pied Piper, moves swiftly to the patio door, all stealth-like, hiding to the side so he can see and hopefully not be seen from outside. Having to swallow another chuckle, I shake my head in humorous resignation. Daria isn't stupid. Shy? Oh yeah, in spades. Dumb? Hell no!

"Food fairy?" one of the guys asks. He's new to the group.

"He means the fa—" Joe sees my deep scowl, hears my low-level growl. "Voluptuous chick living next door."

"The one that cooks like no tomorrow? The one with the food blog, *For the Love of Food?*"

"Uhm-hmm." Getting up to peer through the blinds myself, I check to see if she has had enough time to make it back to her house. If she's moving at her normal pace or faster, by my count— and by that, I mean counting seconds to measure her paces—she should be clear of my yard.

"Woo-hoo." Clapping adds to the elevated and excited noise levels in the room as enthusiastic guys surge to their feet, eager to see what we are gifted.

"That doll should have been a five-star chef. She's that good," says one of the guys.

"We clear?" Joe asks.

"Yeah, she's safe back at her place. Can see her peeking through her back blinds."

Keep right on peeking. Take a good look. Look all you want, babe. I'll give you a full Monty...later.

We've been playing "Peeping Toms" since I bought the

place—actually, since I viewed the property as a potential purchase. Saw her, snagged the house. Aiming to snag that beauty. Might sound a bit creepy. In truth, it's kind of silly. We're both attracted to the other, but for some reason, there is a wall between us neighbors we can't seem to tear down or break through. I think she may be game. Lord knows, I sure am more than eager to progress to the next level. She's a shy and reclusive introvert. I'm afraid of frightening her off. This is our way of living our fantasy until one of us is bold enough to cross the chasm and see where we land.

Quickly, Joe retrieves the large basket. The guys gather around the kitchen island counter, where he places it, pushing away the store-bought bags of chips and dip, presliced cheese, and sausage that's been placed out for nibbles.

Like young boys who think they've discovered some lost treasure, we descend upon the offering, unpacking the contents. As a bimonthly recipient of the secret food deliveries courtesy of my shy, buxom neighbor, Daria Roth, I've regressed into a Pavlovian dog. And so have a few of my friends. It's one of the reasons they want to hold our secret book club meetings here at my place.

Got no nosey girlfriend or wife. What I've got is a bombshell of a neighbor who is also an introvert. One who hides away, only making forays out-of-doors to tend her chickens or tend her immense and fabulous garden, depending on the season. Only other time you might catch her outdoors is when it's dark. Like now. A neighbor who loves to cook, giving most of what she makes away. Secretly. At least *she* believes none know. Thing is, we all know it's her.

Today is my scheduled secret delivery date. Heck, I'm not stupid. Made sure I told Mable Meadows, another neighbor lady who lives on the other side of Daria, that the boys would be over tonight. Was certain that Mable would pass the word on to Daria. I was right. The proof is before us. Like I said, I'm not stupid.

"What's it this time?" Kyle asks, coming out of the guest bathroom. Making a beeline to the beer keg, gesturing to ask if I, too, want another. I nod.

"Note says that this here is a party nibbler sampler. Finger foods that can be put out for gatherings and such. Hey, holiday season is here. Might be some good-eats options. Beats this shit we've put out," Joe says, wagging the included note that lists the various items: pigs in the blanket, mini potato poppers, brown sugar bacon-wrapped pineapple chunks, Hawaiian roll ham sliders, grilled chicken, mango and blue cheese tortillas. Joe nearly weeps when he sees the fried chicken and pulled-pork cornbread poppers.

"Don't forget to fill out the scorecard," I remind everyone.

Joe takes out a handful of pens from my junk drawer, plunking them in the center of the counter. He knows the rules.

No cards, no more deliveries. On this, Daria—I mean the food fairy—is a stickler. A few in the neighborhood have been cut off, dropped from the list, delicious deliveries denied, for such a slight. Clarise Morris hasn't gotten over being denied.

Mable and others in the subdivision often hear about it. Clarise was so livid, she's taken it upon herself to use the HOA to go after Daria for any slight infraction of the ordinances she can drum up. It hasn't endeared Clarise to many, but that hasn't put a stop to her catty, juvenile ways either. Too many fear her wrath, afraid they'll be targeted next.

We fill paper plates with Daria's, I mean the food fairy's, offerings before returning to our seats.

"Never thought I'd see you settle in a typical suburban home in St. Charles, Missouri," Kyle muffles around a mouthful of food.

Joe snorts, shaking his head. "Man isn't stupid."

"Huh?"

"Realtor brought him over to view the place. Still got a working farm bordering this side of the development just out back." Joe gestures out back. "Thought Sam might like it, considering he wanted unspoiled land and all. Our boy here walked out there on the back deck, took one good look at the neighbor lady's luscious full moon as she's bending over, tending her garden. That, along with the scent of her pie..." He shakes his head, chuckles.

"Muffins. She was baking muffins at the time," I correct.

"Likes her pie too. He was a goner. Two orgasms, lickety-split. One right after the other. Put an offer on the place right then and there." Joe chokes on his mouthful of food, he's laughing so hard. That should teach him. It takes a slap or two on the back to get him back to rights.

Everyone pauses in their eating to stare at me.

"I like the lady's goodies," I say, shrugging.

"Is that right, Bro?" Keevan asks, scratching his head. "That was, what, near nine months or so ago. Haven't you made a move?"

I shake my head.

"That ain't like you, Son. What's keeping ya? She married?"

Again, I shake my head.

"Humm. Boyfriend or girlfriend?"

One more time, I shake my head no.

"What the fuck, man?"

"Hey, I'm scoping her out. Getting to know her a bit. Slowly. Keeping my eye on her..."

"Spying," Joe quips, chuckling.

Nope, guy hasn't learned. I toss him a glare, which he pointedly ignores.

It isn't spying (or...stalking) when you are truly concerned for someone's welfare. Gotta make sure she gets home after one of her late-night rambles...check the security of her home by looking for easy points of entry and installing cameras and such...

The guys just stare at me agog.

"Waiting for the perfect time. The lady isn't easy to approach, kinda like a baby deer. Skittish. Got to let her get comfortable with ya. Allow her to approach me on her terms…" I say.

"He's waiting to net her. Hasn't found the right opportunity," Joe translates. "Like I said, the son isn't stupid. He'll get his lady in the end."

I smile.

Chapter 1

St. Charles, Missouri, Present Day

Daria

"Morning, darling daughter." Mom's all-too-cheery voice sings out from my cell phone.

I groan. Must be ten o'clock. Mom always calls at the same time. Every day, it's the same chatter and banter. She really isn't saying anything. At least anything I haven't heard—or want to hear. I'm surprised each time that she actually calls. Not sure why she does. There isn't any need for it, really. At least she reminds me that she's taking the time out of her busy morning to check in on her overweight, overlooked, written-off blob of a daughter. Me.

"What have you been doing?" she asks, as if she doesn't know. I tell her the same thing every day, every time she calls.

"Not much." She knows that I work from home as a freelance editor. What I haven't told her is that I also earn an income from my food blog. That has my cheeks flushing. "Same-o, same-o."

"Hmmm. Wait! Wha—what's that I'm hearing?" Her voice perks up seconds after a motorcycle turns the corner.

Neighbor guy. Halfheartedly, I lift a hand in return for him doing the same. Yeah, I see the way he turns to look back at me over his shoulder. Quickly, I turn away to avoid his returning gaze. It would never do to let him see me. See me looking.

Wait a sec. How is it he's seeing me at all? That…This shouldn't be happening. Does he really see me? I double take on his double take.

As one of the species of fat classified as obese, I am automatically a plate of brussels sprouts. Yuckified already before ever being tried or tasted. Given the wrinkled-nose-in-disgust look on first sighting. Pushed around. Repeatedly jabbed. Removed to the side. Fed to the dog if it's lurking under the table. Ignored. Thrown away with the garbage. Written off.

Invisible.

The proverbial elephant in the room or, currently, as in my case, the great outdoors.

Mental shake, back to Mom…

Damn her ears! Sharper than ever. I inwardly groan. Shit. Did she hear that too? Double shit. Or should that be double damn? Knowing her mom radar—Momdar—she probably hears my internal use of profanity too.

"Okay, Mom. Ya caught me. I was just out for a stroll around the neighborhood," I confess.

A white SUV driven by a salon-platinum blonde zooms mindlessly by. The speed limit is a fraction of what she is going. Does it every damn day. Mach one—a speed that seems to be her norm—does *not* work in this neighborhood. Someone could get killed. That is, unless the driver takes notice.

Doesn't she see me? I am nearly in the middle of the fricking road. She's even ignored the stop sign, again. For a two-hundred-fifty-pound, five-foot-four she-mountain as myself, galloping one's way ungracefully to the other side of the road is the only way to avoid getting squashed like this season's pumpkin. I'm practically invisible.

No, wait—I am. Invisible, that is. Strange, that, but oh so true.

Silence greets my words from the other end of the cell phone.

I can hear Mom stuttering and sputtering some mom-love-inspired, inane reply, as if gathering herself while she recovers or recoils from the shock of it all.

"Daria, are you…are you…exercising? Is that why you sound slightly out of breath?"

Grrr. Is that *hope* I hear threaded into her words? It's the seeming disbelief or condescension that has me getting my back up. Never ends well. At least for me. When it comes to exercising, we plus-sized girls are damned if we do and damned if we don't. There is. Just. No. Winning.

"Uhm-hmm. Mom, I know I might not look it, but I'm no stranger to exercise. *Regular exercise*," I emphasize. "I might not be able to compete in a triathlon, but I can…do stuff."

After all these years, the topic of my weight and all its related subtopics still opens up wounds that will leave one hell of a scar, if they ever fully heal. Such is the life of a meaty woman in an age when heroin-addict chic is the hallmark of today's measure of disgusting beauty. And to think, at one time we thought the age of Twiggy was bad. I snort. Audibly. *Damnation*—I'm doing it—live. At least if it gets away from Mom and this topic, I'd do it—damnation, that is. Heard it can be warm down there in the pits of hell, sort of like a summer resort.

Immediately, Mom goes on the defensive. "I wasn't implying anything. It's you who always blows things out of proportion," she argues.

Fat chance.

"But since we're on the subject…Have you tried that new diet

I sent you? You know…Mavis said it did *wonders* for her niece, and she's even bigger than you." Again, hope rings through loud and clear, as does the disappointment.

OMG. How can that be? Someone that's fatter than me? Impossible. Unbelievable. Figures. Can't even do fat right.

I take out my mental pin and begin the process of popping that out-of-orbit wishful-thinking balloon. Her one dream, one desire for her eldest daughter, the one she's been harboring for nearly twenty-eight years, is just that—wishful thinking. A fantasy that will never be real. Not for me and not for the want of trying. Now if it would just stay deflated, we'd get somewhere. Would a blowtorch work better?

"Yes, Mom." Deep, audible sigh. "I've tried it, along with Keto, Metaba-boost, No-Fat-No-Taste-No-Way, Protein Power, Hormone-aid, Hollywood Hell, Starvation, and all the other new and old fad and fancy diets and programs that you've suggested." Pinching the bridge of my nose doesn't help relieve the pressure building behind my eyes.

"Any results?"

Really?

As if hope were a god. Was she even listening? *Enough already, Mom*, I want to screech but don't.

The day I say yes…hmmm…I wonder what will happen?

Oh so tempting, but the moment she lays eyes on me…Cat will definitely be out of the bag, along with the Chicago-style popcorn. Leaving me up the mom shit creek without any protective gear. Like nagging mom-wasp bug repellent and a supersized flotation device. I'd need that to lighten my load when she forces me up onto her scale, not in the privacy of her bathroom but in the publicity of the main room. The place where *everyone's* gathering, because she's been nice and carried the infernal thing in just for little ole me. Yay. Happy hands!

Defeated once again by the greatest warrior ever. Mom. And all it took was two words.

How is it that the female we love the most and disappoint more often than not can cause such love-induced pain topped with a huge helping of guilt? Is it their superpower? What is their kryptonite? Hmmm. This coming New Year's resolution? Figure that out. Use it. Free myself from that she-beast and the emotional cage in which I've been trapped for all of my life.

Back to Mom and the question she already knows the answer to.

"The same, Mom. Always the same. I lose a bit, then nada, zilch. Then it comes back on in spades. I almost fear trying something new or old again. I'd be happy to just coast if it meant never going up a size." Or two. Or three. Or more.

The blasted sun decides to come out from behind its cloud to rain sunshine down on my marching, parading trombone of an ass. Its rays cast my shadow in front of me. Yep, it's me. No mini-me that, but maxi-me. The gods have come to shame me—publicly.

Only a year and a half ago, I was nicely tucked into my Woman Within stretch 18/20 jeans. Now, the woman without that I really am can barely squeeze into a size twenty-six. And I cross my heart, swear to all that's holy and delicious, it was not a slow creep. It was a wake-up-one-morning-and-scream-at-the-blimp-in-the-mirror sort of gain.

I didn't want to believe it. Couldn't believe it. My doctor certainly didn't. Doesn't. Won't. According to him we, the obese, *the morbidly obese*, are pathological liars.

That's why I'm wearing leggings and an overlong, oversized tent of a sweatshirt in that universal slimming color, black. Thank God we call it workout or active gear. To me, it's a lifesaver. It's comfort wear a step up from pajamas. Sneaky garments. One can get away with wearing it to the grocery store, where people at the checkout may be less prejudicial because of what's covering my ass as opposed to what they think is going into my mouth and all too soon will be wearing on my ass. Now that home delivery is getting affordable…

Volume and coverage always make me feel tinier, slimmer, though the mirror is a big fat liar, or a truth-teller. God, I'm having Snow White flashbacks. Am I being naïvely stupid or hedonistically delusional? Fuck.

I mean, donut.

And as for the Prince Charming? No uncovered dick has pointed at me—as a dowsing rod of lust or love—let alone been near me—deliberately—willingly since…ever. *Lie.* Since I wore a firm size eighteen. *Truth.* That was a lifetime ago, or so it seems. Back when I had other dreams, another life in New York City.

When everything was going as planned. Dreams coming true. Hard work paying off. Before dear, sweet Aunt Alphia needed help. Needed me. That world is gone. So is Aunt Alphia. I shake away the gloom that has never totally diminished. Wishing it back won't make it so or make guys interested. Besides, who am I really interested in that way?

Sam Bixby.

Thinking back on the word *fuck*, or on actual fucking…

To me, fuck(ing) is a desired and even a wholesome, totally expandable four-letter word. Whereas *donut*—never four letters, regardless of how you spell it, by the way—is a blasphemous word, according to the calorie-counter manual, a Bible to all seeking to be less than ourselves, of which I possess no less than three—presents from Mom—in different print versions. Thus, *donut* should be used as profanity, along with chocolate, pie, cake, cookies…

"Mom? Mom, you still there?" I ask after realizing I've gotten lost in my head once again.

"Maybe you should see a doctor, a specialist," she suggests for the umpteenth time.

"What for? I already know what they're gonna say. Eat less, work out more. The age-old battle of calories in versus calories out. Get up off your ass. You're as thin or fat as you wanna be."

"Attitude," is Mom's quick, terse admonishment.

"Realist," I reply in a similar singsongy voice, borderline disrespectful.

Before she can reply, I bulldoze my way to what I hope will end this chronic topic of criticism. "Mom, I've decided on a different approach. I am dieting diets."

"Huh?"

Chips and dip! "Giving them up, Mom. Decided to embrace the bulge and work on health. I might never be lean, but I can still be a mean, eating-clean, fighting-frappuccino machine."

"Well, Daria," Mom begins in that resigned tone she and other mothers get when their daughters either won't listen to their words of wisdom or have succeeded in disappointing them once again, "you'll do what you want. In the end, you always have, regardless…" She ends with the sigh of the motherly martyr she's always been.

"Mom, is there another reason for you calling?"

What the cupcake am I thinking, asking such a question? I want to stick a deli pickle in my mouth or kick myself, but I'm too afraid of looking silly if one of the retired or work-at-home people living on the block peeks out their window. Inwardly, I begin praying that she'll say no, or else I'll have to resort to the "dead zone" trick, as happens with cells.

"Oh, how silly of me," Mom exclaims. Meaning, *Yes, but I couldn't help berating my daughter about her body, again.* "Bunny's son has moved back to the area, though it has been several months—"

"No, Mom!" I cut her off. "Don't. Go. There."

"Then at least come for dinner this Saturday. You rarely come over anymore, and I happen to know that you hardly get out…"

Wait. Back up. How the chocolate soft serve does she know that?

"…which is why I am *thrilled* that you are power walking. Outside. Your father will be so delighted when I tell him." Barely taking a breath, "Speaking of your father…He and I would both enjoy spending a bit more time with our daughter," she wheedles.

Really? I only live twenty minutes away. She knows where. Not my fault she never comes over, even when I've invited.

"Fine, Mom. Dinner. This Saturday," I concede. "Just email me with what you'd like me to contribute."

"Since you're coming with dinner and all, why don't I make you an appointment to get your hair and na—"

"Bye, Mom. Love ya!" I end the call, post the dinner obligation on my calendar, then turn off my cell. Groaning.

Note to self: Leave the phone at home when you decide to leave the house.

At least when walking around the block, I amend. *No, silly. Try checking the caller ID*. Yeah, that could work. Scratch that. She'll be royally pissed at me having missed her call. Donut.

For a moment, I stop. Halt my walking as I review the call. Something about it smells…off. Wrinkling my nose and shaking my head, I continue on.

What was I originally thinking?

Ah, now I recall. Who would have thought that a December day could be this nice? Instead of cold with a chance of snow or ice, it's unseasonably warm, with sun and bright blue sky. The sun is heating my back. Soon it will blind me as I round the circular loop that defines the layout of the modern-style suburban subdivision typical of the area in which I live.

In what was once a field where cattle roamed and corn grew in stately rows, now rows of ranch or two-story, cookie-cutter homes have been constructed, too close together, on postage-sized yards. Not mine. Sure, the front facade is the same: faux-brick front, with the sides done in shades of beige or gray siding. Some come with, others without, fireplaces—I've got three. Two-car garage. Standard shrubs out front. The similarities end there.

It's the interior of my home and the size of it and the lot that are different. Kinda like me.

I've never really conformed to society or Mom's standard of beauty. I try to blend in but never seem able. So I've had to hide what I've kept inside, what lays in back or beyond, where most can see. I've caught a few peeking, even more trespassing. Bordering neighbor guys Sam Bixby and Jim Meadows usually shoo them away. I even let a few gawkers inside and around back. Only a select few.

I inhale a deep breath. Scenting the crisp wintery smells that come with the season, I can detect notes of earth and moisture, a sign that nature is confused. Should the ground awaken, coaxing things to grow? It's all too soon. The warmth. A slight breeze tousles my hair, as if some playful fingers are teasing and tugging at my hastily banded locks.

Feeling trapped and a bit of ADHD-induced boredom, I talked myself into naturally absorbing some vitamin D by taking a walk around my suburban block. Sidewalks create perfect circular inner-subdivision walking paths, one on each side of the street. A third defines the outside perimeter of the entire subdivision, dividing it from the major public roads in a crescent shape of sorts before fading into the remains of a working farm.

The beauty of working from home, at least for me, is that I can set my own hours. As a freelance editor, food blogger, and writer, pacing—along with placing one's self on a schedule—is key. Inspiration even more so. Got to be disciplined to make it work. Which for me means going with the flow.

There are days that I work in excess of twelve hours. On other days, time spent behind the computer is minimal, giving me time for housecleaning, gardening, and reading. And then there's the other important stuff, like researching and experimenting, which requires testing, meaning creating and tasting, new trials, and more testing…which leads me to the persistent and present expansion of my waistline, bust, butt, arms…Don't get me talking on my inner thighs.

Shh, I'm a closet—in my case, extreme, introverted, homebody—food blogger. *For the Love of Food* is the name of my blog. Something I do in secret. Secret from family. They haven't a clue. My few friends don't know either. Or anyone else that knows me. It's a secret. Nobody knows. Okay, maybe I've told a few people, but not many.

My blog isn't just about posting what I've eaten or pics and recipes. I like to explain the history behind the dishes and the origins of the special highlighted ingredients. Debate the merits of different recipes. Discuss what sides should be paired with it, along with the appropriate wine or beverages. All this is accompanied with the recipes, cooking instructions, and ready-made shopping lists, as well as a guide on where to get the more unique ingredients. Plating is important. Posting pictures is a must. Scorecards for each dish and their variants can't be overlooked.

"Mid-America's test kitchen," Mable exclaimed when I explained it all to her. Hmm. I rather like that.

Though it sounds simple, there are lots of hours of hard work behind the few minutes of joy I gain sampling and reading how others have responded to my posts. That is where a few of my neighbors have come in handy. Otherwise, by now, I'd be my own zip code. Some have become my unwitting and unknowing guinea pigs. Others are full coconspirators, like Mrs. Mable Meadows and her husband, Jim, next door. Each secretly delivered dish comes with its own questionnaire and a comment card; once completed, it is to be returned to the basket and placed back outside ready for pick up. This, too, I do discreetly. Covertly.

Unbeknownst to my family, a.k.a. Mom, this passion has brought me a steady stream of growing income. So much so, I can be selective about accepting editing jobs. By prudently investing income and savings—something doable online—I live a financially comfortable life. No millionaire, but solid middle class.

Such financial security has made way for another compelling passion—writing. As a published author. I have four traditionally published contemporary romance novels, with a fifth soon to be released. All written under my pen name, Sonsy Falstaff, a clever use of two synonyms meaning "fat." If all goes well, the income projected soon to be derived from this newest burgeoning passion will more than replace freelance editing as an income stream.

My one guilty pleasure, which far surpasses food, writing, and writing about food—the occasional spying on my incredibly hot, newest next-door neighbor. Sam Bixby. Yum.

To come clean, it began as occasional curiosity but steadily grew while he was renovating the place. It's been growing even more since he fully moved in six months and five days ago after finishing renovations. It makes me wonder why he even bought the place, with all the construction changes he and his buddies have made.

Throwing up my hands in surrender, I admit it. Fine, I'm an urban stalker. Just not creepy—yet, or illegal—much.

I'm thinking therapy might help with that, or at least keep it at bay and within the confines of civil laws. Or time spent between the sheets, or on top, or anywhere else, for that matter, with *him* between my legs. My vibrating wand of a friend helps a little on that score.

The man is one heck of an appetizing dish. One best served… hmmm…any and every *Kama Sutra* sort of way possible, I'm thinking. As long as he's paired with me. Yeah, tantalizingly perfect. Endless options that really should be experimented on and explored. Bet he's got side dishes—don't know, and don't wanna know if he does. Haven't seen any. Don't want to know what has him coming back for seconds, thirds…Sausage knows, *I'd* keep coming back for that…Jimmy Dean.

■ ■ ■

I'm so into my mental ruminations about my yummy neighbor and the rotisserie pleasures to be had, I nearly run into, not over—more like a sideswipe—a pair of midtwentysomething women pushing baby strollers. Double-glazed donut!

As a neighborhood watcher from my office window, and any other window I happen to be near, I've learned a little something about the habits of those that live in and around me. Such as the fact that there has been a spike in retirees and young couples with their first children moving in.

How do I know? No, I don't use the easily reachable binoculars sitting by my computer for such things. They're for bird watching. Can't help it if people get in the way. Often. More than birds. Patterns have developed. Some you can set your watch by. Others let you know what day of the week it is. Helpful when one doesn't get out much. Or when you come up for air after bending over work and the keyboard for far too long.

For instance, I know who watches their grandkids. Who walks. Who walks solo and those preferring pairs and with whom. Know when people leave and return home. When it's safe to place goody baskets on their porches. Who belongs to the runaway dog. Been meaning to get me one of them. A cat, too, maybe.

When spotting Scouts out selling cookies and such, I can warn them off before they reach Irene's front door and even her front walk. I do that by calling them over and placing my own order.

Mean Irene, the crabby old lady three houses down who likes to remind me of the futility of watering the lawn and my garden beds, loudly, from the edge of her twice-weekly mowed grass that she measures with a ruler. Truth. Seen her do it. She loves telling me that her long-departed father was a head gardener somewhere nearer the city, and I shouldn't be watering my plants and lawn during a summer drought, because they'll go dormant. Dead. Is what she should be saying. I know the difference between dormant and crispy. Fudge you very much.

I know a little something about gardening. Learned it from Aunt Alphia, the sweetest lady God ever put on this Earth, now an angel. The reason I came back to the St. Louis area after snagging my dream job in New York City. Someone had to take care of her, especially at the end.

Back to mean Irene. I installed an automatic watering system to avoid the old bat. That showed her. Hah.

Which is why my appearance today is an anomaly. Should have been careful, remembering the time and everyone's schedule. My normal neighborhood walking time, that is, when and if I go for a walk, is reserved for when it's dark and most are in bed. I tend to do stuff when people are more easily avoidable.

"Hello." Trying out friendly. Cheese, I even throw in a wave and smile as I pass them by, as if I do this walking thing every day. As if we're friends. I wanted to be...but not now, not ever again.

My two-syllable, one-word utterance catches them off guard, causing them to startle. Stumble. Stop. Goggle. Yeah, it's me. The neighborhood ghost. The invisible one. The one *everyone* tries to unsee or not to look at if they can't manage to avoid or pointedly ignore me.

We all stop. Nobody is giving way. I'll be a donut dusted in brown sugar and cinnamon before stepping into the gutter. Now what do I do? Awkward.

Abruptly, they cease their tittle-tattle conversation and give me a jaw-dropping look, accompanied by the unblinking eyes of collectible porcelain dolls. *Creeeepy.* One of the strollered kids starts to bawl, resulting in its mother throwing me an accusing glare.

Like, what did I do? Breathe?

As we inch around each other, resuming our walk, going in opposite directions, I clearly overhear their whispering words. "Did you see how *huuuge* she is?"

Yeah, I see myself in the mirror every day. Fudge you very much.

"Forget that, well, her size is something a bit hard to unnotice, considering the shadow she casts," one says in a side-voice share. In a louder side voice, "But, really…what's with that outfit?"

What about it? It's black. Workout clothing. Just like theirs but with more material. Additionally, they're wearing matching zippered hoodies. I'm not.

A good thing about wearing an extra layer of blubber is that rarely do I need to wear a winter coat. So what if I get my stuff online? It's affordable. I don't really leave the house much. It comes to me where I can try it on in shame-filled privacy, avoiding the mortifying stares of the store attendant and her infernal knowing, smirking, yet oh-so-perky question, "Need another size? One or two more…up?"

Don't need to pay ridiculously stupid prices for stuff that gets sweat, dirt, chicken shit, and other real-world stuff on it, like…

BBQ sauce. Uh-huh, *that's* what I've been smelling. Homemade, from scratch.

"Ghastly!" comments the other.

That has me looking down at myself.

Really? Ghastly? A bit harsh, ya think? I shake my head and exhale in wonder. Didn't realize people still use the word. Hmmm.

"Quite right. It isn't even a designer label," one of the subdivision divas says.

Huh, good to know. Wait a sec. Why would I want to wear designer hide-my-ass gear?

I was not aware that there are any affordable big designers that manufacture industrial-sized garments not cut from navy-blue polyester for plus-sized women. True, fashion isn't my area of expertise. On account of my size, clothing shopping has the added terror of reminding me of it. I tend to avoid such things, with the exception of one—Mom. *Sort of a lie.* Outside of her home, we tend to avoid being in each other's presence where circumstances don't dictate otherwise.

"Oh, haven't you heard?" the one twitters to the other. "It's a new shop with several outlets. It's called Sadwill, a thrift store for the fat and ugly."

Hey! I like thrift stores. I can find cheap, cool stuff to use for my food blog experiments. As to the other…Why must it always be fat *and* ugly, fat *and* stupid? As if they are synonyms or perfect pairings, like peas and carrots, cake and ice cream, or chocolate and strawberries. Sex with Sam.

That one has me stopping briefly, before picking up my pace and *before* realizing that doing so will result in having us cross paths yet again on the other side of the loop. Ah, for the love of Krispy Kreme, or better yet, Paul's Donuts, double-glazed and powdered, angel-cream filled, with a side of apricot Danish! Might as well throw in a maple-glazed Long John heavily sprinkled with crispy bacon pieces while I'm at it. Make it two. Never mind. Where's the rabid dog from hell when you need one?

"Shh, shh. I think she hears us." They jig the oops-I'm-so-bad dance before strollering on, with their matching all-terrain baby joggers.

Sometimes you can't remain silent when you've been made an involuntary target. To do so when all parties know that you've heard is license to allow the behavior to continue. *So why can't I do that with Mom? Shut up.* Screw—driver with extra vodka, that old ditty about sticks and stones. Whoever came up with that wasn't fat and overweight.

Stopping dead in my tracks, I turn around to face the female foe. Clearing my throat for the purpose of gaining their attention, I call out, "Fat doesn't mean I'm hard of hearing, ladies," with a high-raised hand wave and finger waggle, before resuming my course. Now both babies are crying. I feel sorry for them—the kids, I mean.

■ ■ ■

Yeah, the two half-dipped Pocky sticks are a bit of what I witness each and every day from my office window. Skinny chicks who dish out cruelty as easily as they whip out their overextended, maxed-out credit cards. Uhm-hmm, that's what they'd been discussing before I *so rudely* blocked the sun, casting a shadow on their parading around the neighborhood.

I overheard, the other day, the one's hubby yelling that he'd found evidence. Go, sleuth. That's right, outside of the monthly statements, he juuust happened to open the trunk of her car, and lo and behold, what did he find? Tons of shoeboxes, not all of them empty. Must have run out of closet space. Either way, busted.

On the next intersection point in the loop, Mrs. Shoe Queen tips her perfectly perky and pert nose up in the air, giving off an audible *harrumph* for my benefit.

Careful you don't get frostbite, I want to say, but that would just be plain mean.

Instead, I laugh like I have a belly full of jelly. Throws 'em every time, and these two…discreet cough…ladies aren't any different.

"Nice shoes, Clarise. New? Hope your hubby found the others worth it. Buy at least one pair of fuck-me shoes?" I hold up a V sign with my fingers. "A vaginal victory may be all it takes to get him over his mad." I give her a wink.

Yeah, she knows I overheard. Hell…*is a summer resort*, and I seem to be booking myself first-class accommodations. I mean, Halloween candy. The entire section of our block heard. First Clarise chokes, then she gasps before turning beet red. Closing my eyes. Not a proud moment, but sometimes it feels so good to let loose.

"Well! I never," remarks Tabitha, her matching BFF, heaving out hot air. Never a leader but definitely a Clarise camp follower, hanger-on, wannabe.

"Rather be fat than stupid, that stupid," I say, turning around to face the foe. "Have a nice day…ladies." Score.

Happy. I waddle the rest of the way home. Which, conveniently, is riiight here.

But they can't leave it at that. When I think all is safe, it turns out I am wrong. Free fudge sundae bar!

"Ignore her. She's nothing. A nobody. Just write off the fat bitch," Clarise's consoling friend counsels.

Free fudge sundae bar—melted.

Like I said before about sticks and stones. Those words score, drawing psychological blood and physical tears more than I want to admit or am willing to allow them to know. Not sure why things continue to hurt. I've had a lifetime building up a tolerance. Still, I find that I'm not immune to such poison.

Still painful. Still lethal.

My back is to them. I blink rapidly, swallowing back anger and tears of such excruciating, agonizing, and awful-tasting, bitter…

Then magic happens.

A strong, solid, muscular male arm comes around my shoulders, curling me into an even larger, robust masculine form. His warmth and scent hit me first. Would it be wrong to push my nose—I could accidentally bump it, or trip—into the nearest part of him, or any part of him, for that matter? Musk. Male musk. Leather. Citrus. Sandalwood. No patchouli here, thank God.

Aww.

Chapter 2

Daria

Yummy neighbor guy. Sam Bixby. I can identify him by smell alone. Uh…from his outside dryer vent when it's going. Drifting scent on the breeze that blows my way. That's how I recognize it, and him. And the aroma that wafts out of his open bedroom window. But it's not to me he speaks.

"Hey, Clarise. Hey, Tabitha." His voice is just a bit too cheery to be honestly nice.

That has me peeking up at him from the corners of my eyes. Huh? What's he up to? Did he hear our brief exchange?

"*Meow*," I mewl ever so softly.

The ever-so-slight twitching and quivering corners of his up-turned, full(-y lickable) lips aren't the only indications that he's heard.

"*Grrr, ruff,*" is his reply.

His nose practically burrowing in my hair, his lips dangerously close to nibbling distance from my ear. Not. A. Problem. I can help with that. Let me lean in juuust a bit…in my dreams.

I am stunned into momentary paralysis. Is this dream whip of a male coming to my aid? Me. Protecting me like the growling guard dog he sounded off? Wow! I can feel him trying to see and read my expression.

The twin stunned looks coming from Clarise and Tabitha suggest that I'm not the only one trying to grasp what the peanut brittle is happening.

"Hiii, Sam," the two skinny bitches reply in harmonic unison. Oh, now they're giving him those coy and flirtatious, well-practiced poses and smiles.

I roll my eyes. Do they even remember *they* are married? With babies?

"Out walking with my voluptuous and bea-u-ti-ful neighbor, Daria?" he asks, playfully bumping me with his hip. He already knows the answer to that. Do they know that he knows? Did he just plant a kiss on my cheek? Bitches glower. At me. Sunshine on a cloudy day.

"Nooo..." I release a how-absurd-is-that laugh "But the two of us are out exercise-walking with our babies. Our paths just happened to cross, twice." Clarise's eyes harden ever so slightly, and her lips pinch before she giggles.

Hey, not my fault. It's called math. Oh, right, the subject she isn't very good at. Got it.

"Want to get back to our prebaby weight. Tone and get rid of what's left of the preggers belly and blubber." She tosses me a smirk, patting her flat abs.

Yeah, I get that too. Even pregnant, with a litter of whatever offspring her kind give birth to, she'd never come close to matching my weight.

Two slices of the best NYC cheesecake, any flavor, that's what I'd give for a good look at Sam's face right now. His hold on me tightens. *Tightens.* TIGHTENS. Combining feigned boredom with waning interest, I weakly hum-sigh and smile insincerely.

"Can you believe it?" Tabitha gushes. The *OMG, not* expression on my face causes her to stutter in confusion before continuing. "Clarise left the hospital ten pounds *lighter* than her pre-preggers weight." She, too, couldn't let that one pass. Marshmallow fluff, she even flares her nostrils as she pointedly looks my frame up and down from head to toe.

I actually like those two end points. I wear a size six-and-a-half or seven shoe. The one small and delicate thing about my frame. Try that on for size, Clarise!

As for my hair? "Your one true beauty." Mom's one, constant positive comment regarding my physicality. Don't know why she's always wanting to schedule me an appointment at her salon.

Yeah, I have to admit, I like it too. Full head of thick, silky, and slightly wavy hind hair. Hind hair: the color of a deer's coat. A mixture of red, brown, and blonde for the most part. The weather and my health can emphasize a particular tone, making it appear more auburn or russet, chestnut brown, even a golden blonde. Goes well with my chocolate-brown eyes.

Sam's arm leaves my shoulders. Visibly, deliberately, and slowly caresses down my round frame, anchoring me to him at my waist, firmly and purposefully pulling me against him even tighter. We three bitches of the block blink synchronously. I hold my breath, waiting for the punchline that never comes. That leaves me even more shaky. Uncertain. Confused. Light-headed from lack of oxygen.

Fear of fainting has me gripping tightly the back of *his* black shirt. His free hand dips behind his back, patting my hand reassuringly and then grasping it in his. He's holding. My hand.

"Well, be careful with that," Sam says.

Double take time. Huh? All three of us females blink at him like we're stumbling on a deer eating meat.

"There is such a thing as being too skinny. A man wants to

know he holds a woman. A real, all-natural gal. See and feel her luscious curves. Got to know he's holding a fully mature female. Can be hard telling with slimmer females. Unhealthy. They feel less fully developed and grown, less a woman and more like a teenybopper."

His wrinkling nose. Adorable.

The looks on them skinny bitches' faces? Priceless.

"Gosh! What *is* that hypnotic smell?" Sam breathes in heavily, raising his own classic nose into the air to dramatically sniff, as if tasting the air. "Smells like…"

BBQ sauce? Melting chocolate.

"Pie!" I yelp. "Oh God—iva chocolate, I left it in the oven baking as I went for a walk," I mumble-screech, breaking free of my luscious dream for saving the probably burned and ruined reality of what has always been my constant source of joy, sorrow, and pain. Food.

Will it ever be my liberation?

Heedless of the staring or talking left in my wake, I rush toward the garage door.

"What kind of pie?" Sam hollers.

"Mixed berry."

"Ladies," Sam tosses out his goodbye. I hear the slapping steps of his pursuit. Of me.

"Hey, Sam?" Clarise calls out. "You coming to the block bash this Saturday? We're hosting…"

Burned-to-a-crisp pie goo that coats the inside of your best baking oven! The block bash is a monthly meet-and-greet-your-neighbors ritual, which I've never attended because, well, I've never actually been informed, save for by Mable, informally. Seems my invite gets mysteriously lost in the mail, both electronic and Uncle Sam's, or the flyer simply doesn't get tucked securely in my door.

Drats. Must be that wind vortex that constantly swirls around my house and none other.

Hmm. Block parties could be fun. If people weren't so…so mean.

My pace slows. I fumble with the garage code. Deliberate stumble with the doorknob leading farther inside. The stalk… uh…jammer in me wants to hear Sam's reply.

"Sorry, Clarise. No can do. Got family obligations," he says absently yet firmly over his shoulder in unstopping strides.

I glance back just long enough to see Clarise's pouty face. Not one to be caught gawking, I make it through the door with Sam still hot on my ass.

Yes, be hot for my ass.

Back and said ass to him, I close my eyes in my desperately desperate, silent plea. The gods owe me, chocolate truffle!

Chapter 3

Daria

Warmth and the sweet aroma of baking assail my senses upon entering my home. My sanctuary. It helps to fool myself that those are the reasons for my now burning red cheeks. Making a beeline to my pie-baking oven, I fling open the oven door.

"You've got two ovens?" Sam's curious voice is clearly coming from behind me. He's entered and is closing in.

"Nope. Four. This double-stack and two oven ranges," I say, indicating the location of the two commercial-grade units. One of the double-stack is reserved solely for the baking of sweets.

"Careful, don't burn your creamy skin in your haste," Sam warns with a concerned hiss.

Creamy? That has me halting mid–pie extraction. He's come nearer.

"Is that how you got this?" He touches ever so lightly the crusting burn on my left wrist.

"Not from baking but from pan frying. Oil splatter."

"Jagerschnitzel?"

The most recent secret delivery.

Flaring nostrils, arching brow, twitching lips, and slightly angled and turned head tell me my game is up. Sonofabutterscotch. I slowly nod. "Presauce."

He leans in, whispering, "Delicious." Warm, moist breath causes a prickle of gooseflesh to rise over my skin. A quivering runs up and down my spine before settling in a warm, moistening oven of my own.

Goo Goo Cluster, I'll be jellied in the knees, collapsing like Mom's holiday Jell-O mold if he kisses my booboo to make it feel all better. Barely catching myself, I manage to keep from thrusting my wrist toward his beautiful face and luscious lips. Knowing my luck, I'd probably strike his jaw and knock him out cold. English toffee on steroids. Nuts!

"Here, let me get that." Sam comes to my rescue once again, hip-butting me out of the way. With two dish towels in hand, he pulls out the golden, flaky-crusted berry goodness, setting it on the cooling rack positioned ready and waiting. "There. Picture perfect," he concludes with a decisive nod after carefully examining the pie product of my research and labor as if it were some culinary masterpiece reserved for the Louvre of baking and cooking creativity genius.

"To be determined," I reply carefully, rotating the very hot, bubbling pie to view it all around. Pretending the golden-brown, decoratively scored top is his belly, I gently press a finger on the baked-to-perfection, golden crust, testing for firmness. Yep. It'll do nicely. Perfectly ton…done.

"What could possibly be wrong with it?" he demands, defending the pie. He narrows his eyes on where my lower lip is tucked inward, presently being gnawed like last year's jerky.

Question asked, said lip retreats and is soothed by my tongue. Wishing it was *his*.

Hoohoo, hoooo. Saw it! The ever-so-slight widening of his eyes lingering on the spot. Juuust to make sure, I repeat the licking part. Yep. That's got his attention. A tidbit to put in my considerably expanding *Sam the Man, Sam I Want* file.

"Well, once it cools, how will it hold up? There is the, ah, initial, ah, penetration of the knife. You know. The first slicing. Will it insert with little effort or tearing of the pie skin, cut clean all the way through? Will the knife extract clean or come away with sticky and gooey"—gulp—"berry bits?" Sam's eyes roam down to where *my* pie is definitely bubbling over. Did he just sniff? At me?

"Will it bed well...I mean, plate well? How will it...hmm... taste?" Holy berry pie, he just licked his lips and flared his nostrils.

"What? Worried about its sweetness or...tang?" he says in a husky male voice.

"Uhm-hmm." I nod, not trusting my vocal cords. My cheeks turn a raspberry red. "Will it serve up well and taste better plain or with additional cum...cream...ice cream?"

That causes the slow lean and descent of his curly, licorice-black hair coming my way to bounce back up. Where was he going with that face? Peppermints. Wintergreen. His breath smells of wintergreen peppermint. Should have allowed him to finish that slow descent toward me. He pierces me with his ombré, corn-flower-blue eyes.

"What kind of ice cream?" Whispers of huskified words enter my ears.

Has it gone suddenly hot in here? My throat feels parched. Maybe from all that salivating over the two-legged, walking and talking five-course meal.

Clearing throat. Testing, testing, one, two, three. "Well, there you go again. There are options. For me, there is simply no contest.

Homemade, for sure—" Squeaky finish. Saved by his excited interruption.

"Homemade? As in *your* homemade? Made by you? Here?"

"Freshest ingredients, combined together into magical, creamy goodness in my own personal, private…err…churn." Drawing his eyes away from my hooha toward my woohah professional chef series ice cream churn.

"God, woman! You got one of these babies here? In your home kitchen!" Sam nearly genuflects before the god of professional-grade churns. Instead, he caresses the cold, temperamental machine.

I'm wishing it were me. Deep sigh. Score for the kitchen appliance. Prickling up. Yeah, right now I'm a bit jealous of that chrome beauty. But then again, it did bring him closer into my orbit and has him lingering still. I could learn to share. Now, how to draw him in and keep him?

For once, I'm not so scared of being sugar-glass shattered. If I were Earth and he were a meteor of cosmic proportions and we were on a collision course? I'd say bring it. I'd love trying to absorb him. All of him. Even if that means total transformation on my part, like as in totally altered. I'd do it. For the love of food and Sam, I'd risk anything, be afraid of nothing.

Suddenly, abruptly, I've returned from my out-of-body epiphany.

Clearing his throat and shaking his head, he says, "I've only seen this beauty on *Chopped*." He frowns. "You're distracting me, babe." Fierce words match his fiercely bright eyes. "What flavor of ice cream?" Eager puppy expression. Cute. I want him.

"The question is…" I begin, walking to my professional, double-sized freezer, "which flavor weds…uh…marries…hmm, goes best with the fruit in the pie as prepared and baked?"

I take out a few flavors already prepared in small batches. Sam clearly enters my personal space as I begin opening up ice cream cartons, bustling about, setting out the appropriate cutlery and utensils.

"Now this particular pie has a precisely measured mixture of blackberry, blueberry, and raspberry to gooseberry ratio. Now, if I can find quality fruit, I have a hankering to try huckleberry."

If eyes were fireworks…

"I've experimented with various proportions of each. This one, I believe, may be the best." Sam raises a questioning brow. "Just as your"—*gorgeous*—"black hair and"—*spectacular*—"blue eyes go well with your"—*lickable, nibbleable, and suckable*—"olive-tinted skin, different ice creams pair well, some surprisingly fantastic and some not so well, as expected, with other flavors that on their own can be quite tantalizingly delicious."

"And…"

Indicating what I plan on trying, I say, "Here we have your basic French vanilla with vanilla bean bits." I hand him a tasting spoonful from the many I snagged, and he samples. "A safe and good fallback flavor if one doesn't want to be too risky or bold."

Sam's eyes widen at my words.

"By all means," he says, licking the spoon with that…ooh… tongue, "be bold. Let's do wild. Even crazy. I'm game. What choices, then?"

"Lemon or apricot with black pepper…"

"Ice cream?"

"Uh-huh, and I'm just getting started." I watch with approval as he takes a different spoon for each taste test. "Here we have… Let me see…A combo of citrus-clove-ginger…plum, annnd hazelnut. I've got other ideas if these don't work."

Dutifully, as a connoisseur of fine wine might, he samples each one.

"So, what constitutes success?" he asks before swirling water around in his mouth. Swallowing. "Two distinct flavors that you think create magic when placed together?" Good question.

Looking Sam dead in the eye, I say, "Chemistry. That's the basis of the beginning of a fine relationship." I clear my throat. "When pairing two different yet equally, distinctively…"

"Scrumptious."

"*Unique* products."

"Hmmm. And after chemistry has been confirmed?"

"Depends upon the interaction. You know, side effects of the encounter. Are they a perfect fit for each other? Start out well enough, then turn into something less appetizing, needing a quick offering to the porcelain god? Does it leave a bad taste in one's mouth? Does it leave one disappointed? Does packaging matter? The only way to know is to try and see where it goes. Give it a try."

Giving him a philosopher's look, I muse, "I think I'd rather have tasted and failed than not. I firmly believe there is the perfect plate of pie. I mean to find it. I'm not talking about being free with my…pie. I'm actually quite picky about what I sample and who gets to sample my sticky sweet." Need to be shutting up. I can feel my raspberry cheeks morphing into purpling-red hues of plum. Peeking at Sam.

Sam stills at my words. I enjoy watching the parade of expressive responses to my ideas on pairings. A softness enters his eyes that captivates and mesmerizes.

"The ice cream now must be combined with that of the pie. Each one photographed and sampled. Want to be my taste tester?"

Sam eagerly nods.

"I'll eat your pie any which way you serve it. Fill out a complete scorecard, too, if you want."

Zingers.

"Oops! I need to run and get my camera." I point toward the other end of the house. "Don't want to repeat and have to start over at this point. Need to capture the moment as it's unfolding." I hurry to return, not sure how long he will stay or how much he will snoop.

That thought has me slowing my pace. As in dragging my feet and dramatically slowing my steps. Let him snoop. I'll take my time. It'll keep him here longer. Rarely do I have people over, since my first and only attempt was a bust. My home is my one secure sanctuary; few are permitted to enter. Lust for my neighbor is playing havoc, making me tread upon new and uncertain ground. I find myself willing to unwrite the unwritten rules that have been carved on my heart.

Sam has indeed done some snooping. Enough into my cupboards, anyway, to find plates. Those will do for some shots, but I've got others I'll use as well. As I go to retrieve them, Sam continues his investigation.

"Some digs, Daria. This isn't a standard floor plan."

"Nope. Got lucky and bought in when the market took a nosedive. Happened to be when this neighborhood was first under development. Larger lot size was one of my prizes. Got to make a few modifications as well. This area and the master are the most transformed." Aunt Alphia's death gift hadn't hurt. I used it as she intended.

My old-maid, honeysuckle-smelling aunt had left me nearly the sole beneficiary in her will. Outside of small tokens, like a pair of earrings and such, to select individuals, I got the lion's share. It came with the caveat that it had to be put to good use, outside of savings, establishing my independence as a modern woman living by her own means in a modern world.

Out of all the family, Aunt Alphia and I most resembled each other. Not just physically, as everyone thinks and believes, but what lay dwelling deep in our hearts and souls. From first laying eyes on each other, we knew we were kindred spirits.

Auntie A reminded me of a plump, round cookie jar—Mrs. Claus in summertime.

Stories, along with warm snuggles, smiles, and home-baked snickerdoodles, are my first memories of the plump fairy-elf of a woman. We shared a love of the written word and food. To her, I could unburden my soul. She, in turn, gave me solace. It was she who showed me the healing arts of cooking and gardening. Encouraged my imagination, my learning, and my desire for exploration and discovery. So in a way, this home and yard are as much a testimony to her as they are a physical manifestation of my dream world.

"Uh, Daria? Did you hear me?" Humor colors his words. Sam's eyes wrinkle with it.

Blinking the confusion away, I say, "Sorry...You were saying?"

"Your home is not the average, standard two-story with a full walkout floor plan."

True, the size of my home is larger than most in the subdivision. Purchasing three standard lots allowed for that. The main living area and kitchen are not what one would normally find in any of the homes around me. Mine is more a custom build. For starters, the garage leads directly into the kitchen area, not via the front entryway. There is the utility room, opposite a full bath, then a large walk-in pantry flanking the short hallway leading into the kitchen.

The kitchen, dining, and living room areas are all one large, open space. A large island with multiple levels for working, standing, stools, and chairs doubles as the physical divider between the kitchen proper and the sitting area. A smaller, more intimate table and chairs sit in a corner bank of windows. A fully stocked, saloon-style wet bar is located in another corner, the one nearest to the stairs leading to the lower and upper levels.

"Very Tuscan, with its emphasis on stone and wood, rich colors, and select tile. I like the old-world charm and feel," says the Roman god himself. He got it in one. I'm more than impressed.

"I wanted lots of cabinets."

"You got 'em. Wish I'd thought of doing something like this…" He smooths his hand over the finish of one, opening a door here and there to inspect the joinings. "My dad, brothers, and friends helped me remodel in the three months prior to me moving in."

Yeah, I know. I spent portions of my days watching. There was a time after his move-in that he still hadn't installed blinds or learned how to employ them properly. Goody. Got a nice viewing then; still do on odd occasions.

An overabundance of hanging and lower cabinets—some full-length, along with additional work counters—line the walls behind the island. Only the oven ranges and double oven, farmer's sink, and windows break the line. I've gone with commercial, chef-grade appliances instead of the standard issue. I wanted the durability, along with greater capacity than the standard residential variety allows. Plus, I like the look. All under a vaulted ceiling with an exterior wall with high and expansive windows. A door near the fireplace steps out onto a large backyard deck that significantly adds to the home's square footage.

In spite of the darker wood and jewel tones, there is a lot of natural light. I prefer it and rarely flip on switches to light my home once the sun is up and shining.

I get us both fresh glasses of ice water.

"Nice." Sam easily makes himself at home, opening a few more of the cupboards. "Ya got lots of individual-style plates and such."

"Yard saling, thrift store hunts, or estate sale finds are a kind of hobby. Gets me out of the house and walking, and around people. It's a way to find unusual and inexpensive tableware."

"Used in shoots like this?"

I nod.

Sam moves on to explore a canning jar cabinet. "You can all this yourself?" His words are muffled while he dips his head, examining the rows of canned garden tomatoes, green beans, pickles, and various things hidden and stored within.

"Oh, I get help. Mable Meadows..."

He chuckles, eyes twinkling cheerfully. Nobody can resist Mable's charm. He's selected a jar of sweet tomato jam, this season's try using a very old recipe I happened to discover that worked out well.

I shrug. "I like to garden. What I can't or don't grow enough of, I get from local farms or the regional farmer's markets. Manage to hit a few U-pick places too. You can have that if you like," I say, indicating the jar. I'm seeing polite resistance readying to be launched. "Really. It would please me to have you accept it. Take it as a reward for being the neighborhood hero. Saving me from the two wicked bitches this side of the block."

Executing a one-hand flip with a one-handed catch of the jar, Sam sets it on the counter near the door. "Hands down, Daria, you got the best garden in the subdivision. Best food. And I'm willing to bet, the best pie." Sam returns to roaming.

"Thanks," I say in a small voice, tucking my head between my uplifted shoulders. I don't manage to turn away quick enough to not see his frown. Hmm.

His eyes find a stone fireplace and wall-hanging flat-screen. L-shaped couches, a few standalones, and tables complete the area.

"Got a full wine and cheese cellar downstairs in the walkout. I do a bit of home-brewing and a bit of distilling and winemaking when the urge strikes." I toss out a smirky smile. "If you're, ah, interested, later I can show ya."

"Cool." Sam's making his way back to me, coming to stand behind me. His radiating heat warms my body, driving the lingering effects of the earlier chilling ugliness of being so long outside. I look over my shoulder as his breath tickles my neck. In spite of all my nervousness, I like it. Actually, I see myself wanting more of…this. Him.

To hide my blush at being observed and at being watched so closely, I snap a few shots of the now cooled, uncut pie, butt butting into Sam when I bend over for a different-angle shot. The man doesn't move but keeps his eyes glued to my rear.

I manage to convince Sam to stand behind the pie with a fisted knife and fork, sometimes a spoon, held up or resting on the countertop. His black shirt and black jeans make a perfect foil. So would the naked flesh of his upper body. Lord knows, I've seen it enough times while he's been working in his yard, swimming in his pool, or through his bedroom window. I don't have to imagine much.

"Beautiful." Oops, spoken out loud. Monkey bread.

"Here, give me that." Sam takes my camera, shouldering me out of the way, diving right on in.

Yeah, I have to remind myself that Sam also works from home. He has his own security company. Man should know how to work a camera. Between the two of us, we work companionably as the first slice is made and the first piece is removed and plated. Once satisfied that I have enough shots, I cut and scoop, plating the rest, adding various ice cream and combos. More pics are taken.

"Okay, pie boy. Now is when your work really begins," I say, grinning at the look coming over Sam's face. I gesture to the plated and ice-creamed pieces of pie. "Taste. You don't have to eat the entire piece. Sample one, then swish out your mouth with a bit of water, chew on a cracker, and proceed to the next."

As Sam samples, I alternate between taking notes and taking candid pics, unmindful about keeping his face out. Some of those pics I'll reserve for myself. I can crop later.

"Mind if I use a few of these with you in them?"

"On your blog? The one aptly named *For the Love of Food*?"

"H-how do you know?" I gasp, sitting abruptly on the nearest stool. I'm not sure he can hoist me if I faint dead away at his feet. At least here he can prop me on the counter and…

"Hmm. Am I missing something here? Is it supposed to be… secret?" He's giving me a confused look, along with a tilting of his head.

"Well, outside of Mable, you, and me, nobody else knows… who knows me." I grimace with my confession.

Placing his fork down, Sam stands in silence. Considering. "Why hide"—he gestures to me and around—"this? *All of you* and this? People should be clambering to get inside. Yet I don't think I've ever seen a car except yours in the drive." He points dramatically to where we're standing. "You should be hosting cooking parties and classes. But you aren't."

Sam begins pacing and roaming through the space. He's agitated, and that energy is forcing him to move. Stopping abruptly, feet away, he asks, "Why do you flinch when you're given an honest and truthful compliment?"

"Sam…"

"That's what you're doing, been doing? Hiding. Why?" Angry demand colors his words.

"Been spying on me?" I accuse.

Sam flinches before his eyes narrow dangerously.

"No more than you on me, MoonPie woman. Don't change

the course, I mean subject." A few choice words are muttered. "I asked you, why? Why, Daria?"

"Why?" I breathe softly, as if speaking to myself. I face off with Sam. "Why, you ask?" Growing louder, with a stupefied anger of my own. Must I speak the words? Is this my punishment for... enjoying, being suddenly, deliciously, deliriously happy? For once?

Sam nods.

"Look at me!" I yell-groan, gesturing to the whole of me. Stupid tears well up in my eyes. "Take a good look. Are you seeing me? This is your answer. Those two slimbar rice cakes you saved me from get it. Why don't you?"

That gets Sam coming up short. As if I've punched him in the gut, then followed up with a bitch slap. I don't even realize my own expression is a mirror of his. Before I can even blink, I find myself trapped. Pressed between my beautiful dark wood cabinets and the blanketing of Sam's warm, blissfully beautiful masculine body. Two of my three loves combined with a gooey center that I hate.

How can I not notice that he covers me completely? Two of my fantasies come to life. But it isn't. It's a mirage. Or is it? Dare I believe? The full-length body-to-body contact has me frozen where I stand. Popsicle. *Lick me.*

He does.

Sam leans into my space, nuzzling my neck. His tongue darts out, tracing a line of its choosing to my earlobe, flicking it. Barely touching, his lips skim my jawline before hovering over my mouth.

"Just like this space you've created, Daria, you're unique, a one of a kind, for all your attempts to remain hidden and ordinary. Ordinary you'll never be. Want to know why? You're *extra*ordinary. Not vanilla. So special, so intriguing I want to know more, taste, touch, and learn more. I just don't get it...why you hide, so desperately…keeping yourself hidden and locked away when you're so…perfect…"

"Perfectly fat. Perfectly ugly and dull. Perfectly odd. A perfect failure and a perfect disappointment…" I say, turning my head away to hide my tears, my pain, and my shame. Now he knows. At least he should.

Sam pushes himself off me. Already I'm missing his warmth, his secure and solid form. The heat of his sudden raging anger radiates from every pore. It leaves me cold. Masculine fingers rake through his hair, another sign of his agitation.

"Now I'm perfectly pissed," he says.

His biting words have me confused. Crumbling gingerbread house.

"First, that you would say such a thing. Secondly, that you mean it. Every wrong word of it. Thirdly, that you obviously believe such bull—" Clenching jaw, fingers curled into tight fists, he huffs short and angry breaths. "Gotta go. Don't trust myself to say something I may well regret."

I watch in stunned confusion as he storms toward the door in a cloud of anger and frustration, slamming it behind him as he leaves. What a punctuation mark. It's left me as rattled as his words.

Not even before I've expelled the breath trapped in my asthmatified lungs, Sam comes storming back inside. With a vicelike grip, he seizes hold of my upper arms, yanking me forward, crushing me to him before his mouth slams down upon my surprised, gaping lips. Fierce, hot anger—and something more—is the flavor before the kiss begins to mellow and his tongue pierces inside, teasing in a languid game of keep-away. Thrusting in and out, as if to kindle what has been burning steadily in me for six months. Desire. Yearning. Yearning desire.

As abruptly as it began, it ends.

Sam pushes me back, leaving me closed-eyed and with slightly parting and puckering, fish-face lips, until my brain has caught up with my body. Blood that drained from my face floods back, staining my plump apple cheeks a near-crimson purple-plum in hue. Pressing my hands to those apples in an attempt to cool them, I pray that I am not giving a *Home Alone*–ish expression. Not what I want to display just now.

"Umm-hmm. Not as I imagined. Better," Sam mutters, popping his lips, as if tasting any lingering flavor of the kiss that may be sticking to them.

Huh? What? Sugar sprinkles of hope sparkle down in my soul, nudging open my heart a crack. Do I dare open that long-locked, dead-bolted, and left forgotten, bruised, and battered organ? Do I take a chance, take the risk? What am I really asking myself? Saying?

Then those piercing blue eyes shish-kebab skewer me silently in place. Only my winded lungs seem able to move. Then they, too, close in heavenly delight as his face lifts to sample the air around us.

"Delicious pie, babe. The mixed berry," he says, dipping his head, lips tickling lips, "and yours." Male lips are sliding to my female ear. "That's what I smelled, then"—head jerking toward the driveway and the earlier showdown—"and now. You can use any pics we've taken," he absently says, standing straight and oh so tall.

Intuitively, I sense that there is more he is not saying, or at least wanting to say. I watch his inner battle on what words will be the next to leave his mouth.

Please don't be cruel. Please don't hurt me.

I don't want the dream ruined. It's all I had before this faster-than-the-big-bang imploding day. I'm rerunning the *Willy Wonka* line in my head: *"We are the music makers, and we are the dreamers of dreams."*

Strawberry shortcake, it's no longer enough to do little more than dream. I want to feast. Feast on life. Real life. And that includes, requires, Sam as every course. But old habits are hard to rid oneself of. Dreams are all I have ever had to comfort me, besides the yummies I can shove between my lips. If not those, if not a chance at Sam, then what?

Capturing my chin, he holds me still so I have no option but to look him dead in the eye. "Just because Clarise and Tabitha are idiots and stupid with jealousy when it comes to you"—Say what?—"don't...don't be so quick to write yourself off."

My feet are stuck in thick caramel sauce.

Back to the door he marches. Stopping. Pivoting. "You, Daria Roth, have tons of worth, more than they ever will. Maybe that explains the size of your human husk, which you seem so keen on keeping hidden and concealed. Ever consider that?" Spearing me with his lethal blues, he isn't finished. "It requires more because you are so much more, have so much more inside you than most. They know it. What's more, I know and believe it. I'll prove it to you. The problem facing you. Facing us. That has me so pissed right now..." His fisting hand rises, reaches out to me. Fingers unfurl. "Daria, *you* are the one that doesn't seem to realize it." Without releasing me from the shackles of his eyes, he snatches up the jar of sweet tomato jam. Then he's gone from my kitchen, from my home.

Alone I remain. Stoically standing. Stunned.

The sound of my breaking heart is only barely muffled by the sound of his motorcycle engine, telling me Sam is really gone. I've lost him before even really having him. Hope, sugar sprinkles, crushed. Blowing away. Candyland destroyed.

I'll prove it.

Chapter 4

Daria

The mixed-up mixed-berry pie affair that started so interestingly with Sam—before the sugar overload precipitating his obvious display of a hyperglycemic rant—is a smashing success. That is, with my blog subscribers. A freak sugar rush corrupting sense and sensibility is the only way I can rationalize what's happened.

That explains Sam.

What explains me is much more simple in its complexity. Lust. Dreams. Lustful and lust-filled dreams with no bearing in reality. Lust-filled dreams smashed into a sugary powder of no amount the millennia of Earth's compressing power can make solid. Never to be rock-solid. Never to be a crystalline diamond. Like I ever had a chance.

Once again, I've allowed my dreams to make a fool of me. In public...well, in the privacy of my home, but in the company of a man. Not just any man, or any male, at that. A really great guy. A really nice guy. My neighbor, no less. Sam.

I must say, after he left, I held up. Like cotton candy does while pouring on hot fudge. Devastated devil's food cake.

Immediately after his departure, I bolted the door and drew all the blinds with a touch of a button, all before running back to my bedroom, crying, weeping, and blubbering. The dark cocoon of my innermost inner sanctum of rooms soothed me somewhat as I lay thrown and prone across my Tuscan-style, dark wood, heavily carved king bed.

After ridding myself of all tears, rolling over, and getting out my fully charged vibrating friend, I give relief to other tense muscles and bottled-up, unfulfilled desires in another way. Totally spent, I lay there, trying to figure it all out.

Since none of it really made sense, and that made more sense than anything, I got my cream puff butt of an ass off and out of the bed, washed, then took myself off to the office to blog and write. Write and blog. Continuing well into the night and early dawn. Noting when the sound of a motorcycle announces Sam's return home.

Guess he's not getting any sleep either. The purring motor lingers right out front of my office window. All the while, I pretend to be otherwise engaged. I have somewhat of a life too, you know.

Taking up Sam's one solid offer, I use a few carefully cropped pics taken of said mixed-emotion, mixed-berry pie with Sam. I post my pie episode. All the standard ingredients of regular posts are included. Much of that work has already been completed. Had been waiting for the baking results. Now that's done...

What's new are the numerous pics that include parts of Sam. Sam's hands bracketing a plated piece of pie in a ready-to-eat pose. Sam's lower face with lips parted and mouth open, a fork laden with pie poised for insertion. Sam's tongue capturing loose bits of pie to save them from disaster. Sam's wide-open eyes expressing delicious delight. Empty plate with finger swirls through purple-red smeared berry residue. Always the sign of a good eat.

Almost as soon as the blog is posted, comments start coming in. A few go like this:

Comment: Great pie. Who's the guy?

Me: Primary taste tester. Has great taste…in pies, among other things. Hero. Willing to save my a** from too much pie-filled calories. Able to leap mounds of ice cream in a single afternoon.

Comment: How much did the taste tester, superpieman taste and sample?

Me: He sampled all there was to sample, in all its variants and forms. Until he couldn't take it any longer. What a trooper! Translation: an entire mixed-up afternoon filled with mixed-berry pie and assortment of odd ice creams. Not enough to make him sick. Just enough to question one's sanity, his and mine. Thinking it was all a dream. Sugar rush outburst notwithstanding, he can eat my pie anytime he wants.

Comment: Great hands and lips on the guy in the pics. What else is yummy…about Pieman?

Me: Everything displayed and concealed. Total package. Disappointed—no. Never that. Confused—habanero hot yes.

Comment: Flavor profile of the dish?

Me: Bursting. Full-bodied with a virile yet natural, heady aroma. Bold. Willing to take risks, at least where flavor pairings are unusual. Of which some are…confusing yet intriguing if there is ample preparation and reflection. Appreciative of quality kitchen appliances and their many uses notwithstanding. Refreshingly brash and eye-opening in a mouthwatering yet stunning, jaw-opening, knickers-in-a-twist sort of you-just-sliced-deep-into-my-heart sort of way.

Comment: What's the next dish he's helping with?

Me: TBD. Still cleaning up leftover pie crumbles. Unbelievable how they keep surfacing. Too many brushed under the rug for too long. Gonna require a bit of housecleaning.

Comment: Red rover, red rover, do you want him back over…to eat pie…humble or not?

Me: Simon says—Yes! He can eat my pie until I die. Working on cookies. He's welcome to try those. Sticks and stones may break my bones, but his words will never really harm me. Confused—yes. Might need therapy. Got suggestions?

Next posting? Holiday cookies. Tis the season, falalalala, and all that. I'll be taking a mixed sampler to Mom's come Saturday. Festive. Criticism-inducing, but in the spirit of the season, so said admonishments and reminders could, but won't, be kept to a minimum.

"Don't want to overindulge on the calorie-laced sweets, Daria." As if I need a DCC—designated calorie counter—particularly when in the company of others.

The real hero of the rest of the day? Mable.

■ ■ ■

The discreet knocking on the front door announces her arrival. Just like each person has their own unique-sounding footsteps, so, too, do they have their own personal knock. Mable knows my rules as they apply to her. She can enter at will.

"Yoohoo, Daria. It's meee. Mable." She singsongs her way in. Part of her signature Mable-ness. "Been smelling something good being carried over from your place on the winter breeze. Had the windows open. Airing out the house, you know. Couldn't help myself with this unusual warm December weather. Regardless, a good airing out of the house during winter will keep the body healthy, fit, and strong. Jim went down to the library. Says it's warmer there than inside the house just now. Gonna find himself some peace and quiet and read the paper for free until the kids get off school and terrorize the place..."

One of the things I enjoy about Mable is her constant monologue, mostly filled with her poetic witticisms and sage advice on how to live a full and bountiful life. Some in the neighborhood are put off by it. Not me. It fits Mable to a tee.

"Nothing wrong with your nose. You've been smelling mixed-berry pie, Mable."

"That's not all I'm sensing. *Saw* some rather interesting shit going down. *Smelled* it too; thank goodness for the sweetness floating from your house before the sources moved on. *Heard* some rather interesting gossip. Then, seeing that rather good-look'n Sam Bixby hop on his motorcycle just after leaving your place got me wondering..."

"Come sit yourself down, Mable. I'll pour us a cup of coffee, slice us each a piece of pie, and you can fill me in."

Not sure how she does it, but Mable is a virtual font of neighborhood gossip and inside intel. There's not a mean bone in her body, but she has a heck of a lot of information on everyone and anyone.

For the next full pot of coffee, each with a slice of pie, the rest wrapped and set aside for her to take to Jim, she does just that.

"And you got all this from Clarise and her bitching buddy Tabitha?"

"Heavens, no, child." She deep-throat chuckles while waving away my silly statement. "Irene..."

"Mean Irene with thoughts of how to keep things green, which actually will make them fry and die, Irene?"

That catches Mable off guard. Inhaling a breath, cup poised to lips, she actually has to think it through. Mable's laugh begins as one of those throat squeals that morphs until it's a full-on rolling display of true, appreciative mirth. One of my hens, Penny, makes those same sounds.

Mable and I have been coffee-drinking buddies, gardening buddies, and sharers of the finer points of food, men, and general domesticity and other mundane and helpful hints sort of buddies since the day we said our initial hellos. Mable and Jim (by extension) are the only ones, outside Sam's great reveal, who actually see something of me. Speak with me. On a regular basis—simply because they want to. As if I am truly a person of worth and value.

Mable has never written me off.

Seems Sam hasn't either—yet. Or has he...now?

I am glad for Mable's company. Even gladder to see the rest of the pie go. Reminders of poisoned and confusing moments tend to linger too long in my heart and soul, not to mention my brain. I sense another disturbed, sleepless night approaching. Sam's pie, as I now have dubbed the mixed-berry delight, doesn't need to go through my lips more than it already has.

What's one of Mom's favorite sayings? "Once through the lips, twice on the hips. And for you, Daria, that means times four."

"Cute, Mom. As in, 'fatty, fatty, two by four, and with Daria the entire lumber store,' and getting stuck in doors and all that."

With cuts so deep, I never needed to indulge in that form of self-flagellation. Or have I? That thought has me internally sputtering.

Mom loves me. I must believe she does, but sometimes I do wonder. Mom says and does things out of that love, her sense of love. I don't think she understands that what she says hurts me. Has the power to destroy me. Have I followed down that same path? How can I demand that others see me differently, treat me differently, when in my heart I agree with their assessment and treat myself in kind?

My weapon for comfort, as well as self- and assured destruction, has been the one thing nobody can live without. I mean absolutely nobody. Food.

Chapter 5

Sam

After carefully placing that precious jar of Daria's homemade to-mato jam inside the house, I grab my keys and helmet and set out on my bike once more. Fearing I just jammed up something I meant to propel, feeling the wind in my face seemed the best thing to do. Cooling off my mad is one benefit. Allowing time to think, review, evaluate, and strategize is another.

Yeah, I saw her earlier, walking the block. I had to do a double take. That woman, Daria, always turns my head. Gorgeous hair. Serpentine shape. And her ass…Actually, both my heads rise to attention when we encounter that rare one. Granted, it's her bodily form that first got my attention. Discovering more and more of what lay within her, that has me even more riveted.

If I have my way, and I mean to, there will be many, many more encounters to come. Eventually, I will be having her. My way. And if today's experience was but a sample…every delicious morsel of her will be mine to savor. Often. Soon. Forever.

I circled back after that first glimpse and double take. Even if I weren't just heading out for a rare winter ride with something important to do, I would have turned around. Needing to see her again for myself. That one is always up to something.

Wonder how others will respond, discovering just who and what is living in their midst. Secrets can only remain bottled up for so long before popping their corks, covering one and all in a deluge of surprise. I'm not sure why so many are surprised when that happens. What with so many having been jerks toward her and all. Here, living only houses away, is a true treasure that few recognize and fewer see. It's like she's invisible.

It was a bit out of character for her to be walking around the neighborhood just then. Daria's a nightcrawler. One of the few that ventures to lap the subdivision after dark. I'd been keeping my eye on her since first seeing her while viewing the house next door when it was up for sale. I kept on looking when purchasing and renovating during the three months before moving in. First time I saw her out walking after dark, I did the gentlemanly thing—I followed her. Discreetly. So what if crime is nonexistent in our part of the woods? Someone had to make sure she was safe. I've been doing that ever since.

It's been about nine months now. Bet I know more about Daria than Daria knows about Daria. After today's encounter, that's becoming all the more clear. Painfully so. For both of us. Since security is my business, I know that there are all kinds of safe. There is also being too safe. Which is why Daria is such a puzzle. A puzzle I mean to solve.

Yeah, I take notice of such things. Daria isn't the only one in the neighborhood to work from home. I run my business and my hobbies out of my home. Convenient, and more common nowadays than one would think.

I knew there could be potential trouble when after passing Daria I passed Clarise and Tabitha. Those two conniving, youngish stay-at-home mothers have appointed themselves the neighborhood dictator-queens, self-appointed busybodies that like nothing more than pointing out everyone's flaws—except their own considerable ones.

Those walks aren't always friendly forms of exercise. Most times they're taking notes, documenting and recording what they perceive to be HOA infractions, infractions that are then reported to the appropriate authorities. Meaning it will soon become a problem for the victim, until there is a new victim in their sights. Those two, along with their husbands, want to rule the neighborhood.

They rule by being mean and cruel. Their favorite victim? Daria. *My* next-door neighbor, Daria. Daria with the largest yard, packed full of plants and planting plots so that it is a virtual botanical garden. Most amazing.

Mable says Daria's turned down requests from people wanting to tour it. I've scared off a few nosy trespassers poking around on rare instances when Daria wasn't home, out helping themselves to cuttings and whatnot. I ended up placing a security system to record and illuminate future garden raiders. Helps me keep tabs on my lady as well. Hey, two birds, one stone and all…

"Meat, medicine, and delight." I heard Daria sharing her gardening aesthetic to a bolder HOA member who bothered to stop and talk to her about it. Strange how few do. Daria, the one who hardly is seen, but all know of her presence by the positioning of her trash cans and the continual maintenance of her yard and the backyard Eden Daria does by herself.

Daria, who raises chickens just on the other side of the proverbial line demarcating subdivision boundary lines with the grandfathered agricultural zone that ever seems to diminish. After the two goose-stepping twins went after Daria's chickens, using HOA muscle to force Daria to get rid of them, the farmer that backs up to our yards sold her a few contiguous acres to keep the HOA off her luscious ass. I purchased the same amount to keep the property line straight. Cyrus's wink told me he wasn't fooled. He said no to all the others wanting a similar deal.

Chickens, you see, are against HOA rules. Newly amended rules. Rules altered when nobody knows or recalls. According to Jim Meadows, who got it from his wife, Mable, Daria was plenty pissed. A couple times I could even hear an occasional rant coming from next door. Windows were open at the time. And I was standing just outside. Outside of her window. Clever Daria found another way to get what she wanted.

"Why didn't she go to the HOA meeting that was deciding the matter?" I had asked Jim.

"Did you go?" he challenged. Hoisted by my own petard.

Shaking my head, I said, "Out of town, but I sent in my vote on the matter."

"Peculiar thing there about that meeting, Sam…" Jim scratched his chin before shaking his head. The man was as perplexed as I. "Nobody can recall just when and where it was held. And saying if it really happened, nobody had the decency of talking directly to the dear girl. Sure, they came around with petitions to sign, which according to Clyde Brown down the way, none but a handfew did, nobody 'members hearing about an HOA meeting being held. Weren't posted."

Yeah, most peculiar.

"An order came by mail telling Daria to get rid of them birds of hers. Why? There weren't any complaints. Weren't no smell. Hens don't make a fuss. Daria made sure she had no cocks about." Getting my stunned attention, cackling at my expression, he explained, "Cocks. Roosters. Roosters crow, hens cluck. Roosters loud. Hens quiet."

He shook his head, either out of humor or disgust for my confused ignorance. The word *cock*, and any idea of her consorting with another male…

"Get good eating eggs from them. Grandkids love 'em. Eat pesky bugs, keep our yards free of many pests that infest the others, and keep the flowers looking prettier than ever. 'Course everyone is more than willing to take the eggs free and help themselves to natural nitrogen-infused, broken-down, and mulched straw for their own plants." Joe made noises of disgust. "Then that Cyrus James, the farmer from out back, got wind of it all. It was he that came around asking if she wanted to place her chickens on his side of the line. After a bit of talking, he sold two acres' worth to her."

"Cyrus James's one of the recipients of the food fairy?"

"Uhm-humm. Don't you know it. Real surprised and pleased as punch, too, when it started up and kept up regular. Even more so after his missus passed. Most pity pots of casseroles and such he just tossed to his hogs. Kept and ate every morsel what Daria gave 'im." He barked out a laugh. "He won't say he knows it's her."

"Why's that?"

"On account he don't want to hurt her feelings, Son. Girl's been plenty beat up, and all on account of her weight. Think she's been bruised more than most. Guess such a life either makes people into serial killers or angels. Ya reckon?"

"How about garden divas and food fairies?"

Daria, the not-so-secret secret deliverer of mystery baskets of enticing food and full dinners. Discreetly placed on my doorstep and that of select others at least once a month. How do I know it's her? Was always her?

If Mrs. Meadows, or her husband, Jim, hadn't squealed, it was my own surveillance system that confirmed it, security systems being my stock and trade. It's my business. I'd be a stupid-ass in spades if I didn't install the latest in that technology in and around my own home. It's a great way to test and demonstrate equipment. It's great for figuring out who's been sneaking baskets onto the front or back porches. Better still, in discovering who likes to watch out their windows at unsuspecting neighbors like me. Yeah, I know she's been watching.

It's a great selling point. "Why, Mr. Ambrose, this is the very same setup I use in my own home. Come around and I'll show you just how it works and how easy it is to operate. If setup isn't your thing, I can get that done for you as well." Usually ends with a sale. I do a lot of corporate work, but home clients are on the rise.

Amazing what you can catch on camera.

Caught Daria. Got a recording of her delivering the first and all the rest of her basket goodies. The first delicious delivery: fried chicken and green beans made with potato, onion, and bacon, along with cornbread. All homemade with a few "variants," as Daria calls them. Complete with scorecards and questionnaires. Each one, including myself and any friends who happen to be over on those delivery days, is diligently filled out. We've become some of her loyal blog followers. DD Day—Daria Delivery Day—has become a regular hangout day at my place. Not sure if she's caught on.

"Jeez, man, ya gotcha a food fairy frolicking around the frigging block?" joked Joe, finder of the first delivery.

The man must have been a hog, one of them truffle-snuffling hogs, in a previous life. He can smell out food anywhere. Root it out faster too. Joe, my friend and business partner, is an all-around nice guy, though he can be a jerk at times. He handles the shop and warehouse and helps manage installation crews.

"What are you getting on about?" I asked, tilting my head in curiosity when he came waltzing inside carrying a large wicker basket.

"Joe, you changing your name to Lulubell Red and gonna start skipping through the woods on the way to your granny's house?"

"Fuck's up with that?" Joe's a philosopher at heart. It shows in his choice vocabulary and ability to express subtle nuances.

"The adorably cute and quaint basket." He looked down at the thing he carried. "Goes better with a skip that's got a bit of bounce, as opposed to your heavy-booted shuffle-stomp. Just a suggestion." I winked. Joe came to a complete stop. Dangerously dark eyes unblinkingly focused on me. Where fools and friends are wont to tread…"Maybe we can find ya a pair of black, patent-leather shoes, white bobby-socks, and a blue-and-white gingham dress? Pull back your unruly, curly mop you call hair into braids with matching bows? Huh? Would you like that?"

"Shut the. Fuck. Up," he growled, slamming the basket down on the table.

Stuff inside started clinking and clanking, getting our attention.

Like two boys at Christmas, we were irresistibly drawn to what lay within. Silence reigned as we emptied out the contents and looked upon each extracted item in amazement. *I do believe in food fairies. I do.* Then it was a rush for plates and utensils.

"Seriously, Joe. You bring this with?" I asked, teeth ripping into the chicken as if I were a Neanderthal. Forget manners. It was only Joe. I sucked off the flavor bits and juice from my fingers. Didn't want any of this goodness to go to waste.

"This fabtabulous feast ain't my doing. Wish it were. I'd make me a fortune food-trucking if so. Nah, man," he said around a mouthful of cornbread liberally smeared with homemade honey butter.

The honey Daria gets from her own hives. That was another run-in with Clarise of the HOA. Another win for Daria.

Joe kept eating, but his words got me stopping. Choking.

"Then where did it come from?" I asked.

He gestured toward the front door. "Out on your front step. Someone must've left it there."

"On purpose?" I gulped. My throat began a spasmodic dance.

"Note don't say. Says, 'Welcome to the neighborhood, enjoy.' Which I'm doing and would do more of if you wouldn't interrupt. Hmmm." He started reading the note, held with greasy fingers. "Fill out scorecard and questionnaire, if we please. Leave all on front porch for later pickup." Shrugging, he went back to eating with relish. "There any dessert in there? Guy's gotta know how to pace himself if there's dessert," he defended himself.

All I could do was stare until finally I was able to speak. "Apple tartlets."

That had him pausing, a peculiar grin emerging on his chicken-greased lips.

"We're eating food made by who knows and from who knows where? Joe! Doesn't this concern you in the slightest?" Even my shocked and demanding tone didn't penetrate.

"Nah. Should it?" Chewing. Swallowing. Another bite. Humming with delight. Repeat.

"It could be poisoned..." *Let that sink in, slick.*

At some point, Joe actually paused, considering. Then, shrugging his shoulders, he continued eating heartily. "Well, we all gotta go sometime. If this here food is poisoned..." *Gulp.* "Gonna eat more of it so it works quicker and I go out a happy man." Smiling around a mouthful, he continued to chew.

Wiping my mouth on a paper towel, pushing up from my chair, I beelined it to my security networking closet. Running the saved recording of the front door camera, I reviewed the feed. "Well, I'll be..." Happy smirk, twinkle back in my eyes. Every part of me was interested. "Down, boy," I muttered, shifting my stance while speaking to my overly eager downstairs wiener dog.

With a sigh of satisfaction and delight, I rejoined Joe and rummaged around the basket to see what was left. Plenty. Yeah, if this was a sample of what Daria Roth could cook up and dish out, anyone who dies in her arms is already guaranteed to die happy.

Color me intrigued. I returned to the table while scratching my two-day-growth whiskered chin with pursing lips, a feral gleam in place.

Joe eyed me. "Everything good?" he asked, lightly pausing in his eating.

"Yep. Fine and dandy. All's good. Way more than good." Truth.

We followed the instructions to the letter. More goody baskets kept coming in the weeks and months that followed. I learned that recipients who didn't follow the rules, especially where it came to the scorecards, got dropped from the list. Delicious delivery—denied. One of those? The home of Patrick and Clarise Morris.

"The missus tells it that Clarise wanted to keep the baskets and even demanded a proper menu from which to select her free meal, along with the number of servings…" Jim was laughing so hard in the telling that he could barely finish. "Boasted that she planned her dinner parties around the deliveries, then claimed the cooking as her own."

Late this past summer, another delivery coincided with when I decided to host a party, inviting my biking buddies. We're not a badass MC gang-like sort of motorcycle club. More along the lines that we're a bunch of buddies and friends that like to own, work on, and ride motorcycles.

Not sure how Daria figured the number of those that would be showing. The food that was delivered was more than enough to feed the group of hungry men and a few of their babes. It must have taken Daria several trips to get it from her place to mine. The menu selection—spot on. We're talking BBQ sampler feast. Hog, beef, bird with all the fixings, with a few variants, including peach cobbler and apple pie for dessert. My planned dogs and burgers got tossed into the freezer.

My gang of friends got a real charge out of thinking that I was the one responsible for the food. I let them believe so for a while before coming clean.

Then it was my turn, with their help, to be the mystery wizards of wonder. Most of us are pretty handy with a set of tools and know our way around construction. Heck, they were the ones that helped with my remodel prior to moving in. One of my buddies even put in the in-ground pool I got out back. It was inauguration day for the pool. Plans were to get wet and wild.

Daria got an eyeful. That's for sure.

Yeah, I saw her peeking, spying from various vantage points. I took my time peeling off my shirt in clear and plain sight. Did a slow 360, giving her the opportunity of seeing me all around. It was when some of the guys thought to swim skyclad that she disappeared, only to reappear again, and again.

Later, it struck me hard. There was the lady who'd done all the world of labor and expense in preparing the feast. Me and my friends didn't have to lift a finger or even provide the funds or ingredients that more than filled our bellies. Where was she? Inside. Alone. While the rest of us were eating, swimming, and having ourselves a grand ole time.

"Boys, we got to do right by her," I proclaimed.

I learned from Jim Meadows when Daria was expected to be out of town. A rarity. That's when me and my friends pounced, returning the favor. A gift that would go on giving, and we would continue to be the recipients. Yeah, cheeky and clever on our part. Everyone came out winners.

We put in a backyard kitchen—the works, complete with a smoker, grill, and BBQ pit. Joe insisted we add a pizza oven, putting it close to her beehive bread oven. The wafting aroma from that too often drives me crazy. Its siren smell can draw me out from anywhere, begging for a sample. One I either sneak or is purposely left out, along with fresh butter and spreads.

"Cried tears of joy for days every time she laid eyes on it," Jim revealed. "Rubbed them brown eyes of hers first time she saw it. Old man Cyrus was there too. He saw it, nearly laughing himself silly with delight. Daria couldn't believe it. That girl is one that still believes in angels and fairy tales. Took over an hour inspecting every inch of it. Said she couldn't have planned it better. No finer execution in the construction and what appliances were incorporated. Real appreciative. And don't you go thinking that all them individual cakes and pies and bags of cookies sitting near your back door is any indication that she knows just who's responsible."

"Then why is all that there?" Finding all that sugary goodness of a thank-you was another woo-hoo moment for me and the boys when said goodies were found and parceled out.

"Mable said that you were the one to know who was behind it all, as they had to come through your place to install," he said, placing a finger on the side of his nose, combining it with a wink.

That got me laughing. I won't tell him or Daria that I got the reveal all on disc. Watched it several times, sharing it with the boys too. Sweet.

Yeah, my neighbor is one sweet lady, though she does have a prickly side to her that I like as well. She's also vulnerable. I rev up my engine and shoot down the highway. It's the only way to vent some of my frustration. Damn, did I fuck it all up? This is like one of those soufflés. You gotta be careful about how you handle it lest it collapses. Don't want to destroy the lady, just want to make her mine.

Chapter 6

Sam

"I wouldn't go over there right now, if you're after taking an old woman's advice," Mable whispers in a conspirator's voice, the only thing penetrating my determined countenance. She's caught me on my way over to Daria's.

"Say what?" I ask, shaking my head to rid myself of lingering mental fog. "Sorry, Mrs. Meadows. You were saying?"

"I'm telling you, Son," she whisper-shouts. "It's too soon. At least for her. Daria is too fragile. Still too tender right now. You need to keep your distance for a day or two more. Whatever went down between the two of you of late…" Yeah, she knows more than she's letting on. "…hit her hard. I'm talking devastatingly hard." She wings her knowing eyebrows my way.

Coming up short, now I don't know what to do. With flaring nostrils, raking hands through tousled hair, rubbing the back of my neck, I'm torn. Do I listen to Mable's advice or listen to my own inner voice? If my pecker had his way, we'd be storming her door and claiming her as ours. Now.

"That bad, huh?" I ask.

"Uhm-hmm." Crossing arms. One decisive nod.

Flicking a glance over at Daria's, I happen to catch the quick movement of parted blinds snapping shut. We…I'm being watched. Narrowing eyes on the spot, I wait. And watch. Rewarded. There. Ever-so-slight widening of two blind blades. Pointedly widening my eyes, I throw her a crooked grin, then mouth, "I'm sorry. Can we talk?" Snap go the blinds.

What's the window-blind code signal for yes? No? Go to hell and burn you bast…There she is. Coming out the door. Desperately trying to appear nonchalant. Her face reveals the truth she tries so hard to hide. She's too pale, save for the red-rimmed, puffy eyes. She's been crying. Hard. Over me or because of me?

"Hello, Sam," she says in a voice too thready and soft. She's sniffling. The trembling lower lip she tries stopping by rolling both and pinching together. "This was delivered incorrectly to my address. I believe it is yours…" she says, handing me a package.

How is it that I didn't even notice it until now?

Clearing my throat, I say, "Thanks." Taking it from her, I hear Mable's inelegant snort. I turn briefly to the older woman, who arches one brow and gives me a slight sad shake of the head.

"The box is clearly marked. How'd the driver get confused as to where it should be delivered?" I ask, puzzled by this paradox.

"Mistakes happen?" Daria offers.

"Cookies," Mable chirps, still standing here. Still listening. Intently. Still watching. Like a hawk, or the neighborhood paparazzi.

"Come again?" My eyes focus on the flaming flush that's taken over Daria's cheeks.

"For the love of food. In the case of the driver, it's Daria's cookies. He knows that every time he drops off a package, wrong or right, Daria gives him a homemade cookie. Has a jar of them sitting on a table right next to the door. Daria delivers the package for him later and gives up her cookies with a smile and a cheery wave."

Half mad with jealousy, I snort, "I happen to *love* eating Daria's cookies. Love eating her pie too. Fact is, I love nibbling on anything Daria's willing to dole out. All of it. Never had a bad dish that's come from her kitchen, made by her own hands. There is more to Daria than her cookies. More to her than just her food."

Turning to Daria, pinning her with a steely glare, I say, "If that guy doesn't get it, then you shouldn't open the door to him. You deserve better than a one-note cookie consumer who can't figure out how to get what he wants while still doing his job—delivering packages."

Mable snickers. Daria stands stunned. Her face is doing this strange oscillating, changing-color thing. Alternating between shades of pale all the way through the pinks, reds, and purples. Repeating the process like rotating lights.

Hoisting the package up under an arm, then reaching out to Daria, grasping her hand in mine, I drag her back to her house. "You don't look well. You're coming with me. Get you some tea and maybe a lie-down," I mutter as I usher her up the pretty walk.

Chapter 7

Daria

Tossing glances over my shoulder at Mable as I'm dragged by a determined Sam, I see her winging brows and pleased-as-punch grin. Pressing her age-wrinkled hands to her lips, she then claps with glee, getting a double take. I'm vaguely aware she's skipping, power walking back to her house. Jim's about to be the recipient of more neighborhood intel.

What am I about to receive? Will I be truly thankful? Left wanting more? Is this some answer to my prayers? Or will it be sending him and myself screaming into therapy, seeking admittance inside cloistered communities for an eternity of repentance, washing feet, and serving varying courses of watered-down gruel?

"Sam?" So many questions are packed within the name, symbolizing that sweet cannoli of a cookie pieman.

He's firmly holding my hand, yet gentle. Determined strides match the steel that has taken possession of his cornflower blues, replacing them with a foreshadowing of what may be on the horizon. Bring it. The entire menu, if you please.

I wiggle my hand deeper into his larger, warmer one. The subtle reciprocating squeeze tells me everything will be okay. I'm thrilling from the excitement. Sam knows my move is deliberate, and he *likes* it. Hope glitters through my lashes as I search his face.

Softer voice. "Sam?"

"Everything's gonna be okay, babe. I'm seeing to it. Together, we'll make it work. Let me take care of you. You need me," he softly replies. Still not stopping. Still not looking. Still determined.

"Kay."

How long does it take to walk-march-drag from sidewalk to door in a suburban neighborhood?

The firm shutting of the door blocks out the world but for the two of us. The answer doesn't seem to matter anymore. Nothing and everything seems to matter. All pales when placed beside what is and the truth of what we both want. For me, that's one thing and everything. It starts and ends with Sam. Sam is what matters. He's what I want.

"Sam?"

Dropping the package at the door with a thud, not caring what's inside, he looks around, indecisive about just where to take us from here.

"Sam, are you interested in talking? Tea? Something else?" I raise my shoulders, sinking my neck, a grimace on my face.

Squeezing my hand, he hasn't let go. He's slowly turning his head toward me. Narrowing his eyes in a sideways turn of his head that lets you know he's looking and considering. "Ask what it is you truly want. Ask me again. Without the built-in apology."

"Huh?" I say, wrinkling my nose in confusion and curling my upper lip.

"Ask me again, I said. This time, do it without any expectations of rejection or with the foregone conclusion of being written off."

Swallowing lump in throat, sniffling and waggling my nose, I straighten my shirt and shake myself into some semblance of dignity and forbearance. "Sam," delivered in a squeaky voice. I receive a negative shaking of Sam's head. "Start over?" Nodding.

"No serving up simple vanilla, Daria. This is specialty pie time. Daria pie. Requiring the best of the cream. Try your inner flavor that's bold, daring. Wild."

Hmm. All righty, then.

I clear my throat. Deep breaths. Ready. Squirming where I stand. Not quite ready, then. A quick peek shows Sam's half-quirking grin of anticipating glee.

I can do this. This shouldn't be hard. Isn't hard.

Who am I fooling?

Violet Crumble bar. That's the combo: chocolate-covered honeycomb toffee, airy sweet. The sensation that comes from the first bite, pressing your tongue against the golden honeycombed center...

Placing my hands in the middle of his stomach, slowly, I soothe them upward over pecs and shoulders, lifting up on tiptoes to continue the caress. Looping arms around his neck. Locking myself in place by interlacing my fingers. Pressing further, deeper into his frame. Pleasure erupts inside my wounded heart when I see his wide-opening eyes and hear his slight escaping gasp. Something trapped lower down between us begins inflating. I give him my cat's-got-the-cream-*and*-the-canary look.

"Sam." Silky word successfully executed, softly spoken into his ear. My lips graze the fleshy shell. "Sam, do you have the time?" Tongue flick. Lips a breath away from his. "Would you like to stay for talking, tea, and...me?" Secret-seductive smile successfully mastered. Thank you, YouTube. And the hours of practice behind closed blinds and barred doors.

I push away from Sam, who is standing timber-straight and still. "How did I do?" My hand remains on his chest, feeling his heart, which beats like an electrified kettledrum. I blink innocently while waiting for his response.

His jacket hits the floor with a resounding thud, echoing that of the package. "Yes."

Smorgasbord.

Along with its power to compel people to stay and come back for more with mouthwatering eagerness. No Vegas all-you-can-eat dive, this, but a quality feast set before the gods of yore.

As we push and pull each other down the hallway, Sam pauses. Curiosity flickers. "Did you say something?"

"Did you hear something?"

"Yeah, like, 'all-you-can-eat buffet.'"

Too bright and gay laughter bursts forth from between my lips, causing him to narrow his gaze.

I sober considerably, immediately. "Why would I say something as silly as that?" Deflecting is the art of the avoidant when they've been caught. I learned that one from dear old Mom.

Pulling me to him, running his hand over my hair and face, he tips up my chin. Next it's his lips that trace the edges of skin and scalp. Dreamy as mounds of real cream—whipped cream. Softly, his lips skim flesh that has begun to heat to a brightening pink. "I know I'm going to love discovering your idiosyncrasies. They, like you"—kiss—"are"—kiss—"simply"—kiss and another kiss—"adorable." Eye-popping kiss. Penetrating, tongue-preventing, snappy, unclever-clever comeback of a kiss.

Sam's kisses? Manna.

"Bedroom is through that door," I say lamely, indicating with a finger, hand, and limb that have suddenly lost their ability to fully function. They are acting more like limp noodles. "I'm fast turning into crème brûlée without the sugar-crusted, caramel-y toasted, torched top."

He gives a deep, throaty chuckle of male satisfaction. "Sweet, creamy custard. Tasty. By all means, allow me to sample all the delights that are you." His knee pushes me farther down the hall and into my awaiting oasis.

Once again, forward propulsion is stayed by curiosity. Or is that wonder and delight reflecting from his face? A man's first long look at his lady's boudoir. The master is an area that I had the builder modify, deviating from the standard plans. It's bigger than most standard masters, with stone accents around doorways and windows. Rich earth and jewel tones rule here. As do stately comfort and old-world charm.

The Tuscan-style furnishings were selected for their statement of solid endurance and old-world elegance. Heavy wooden beams outline the tray ceiling, giving the space a more cozy and intimate feel. The stone fireplace is flanked by built-in bookcases filled with favorite titles and curiosities I've collected. Before it sits a plush seating arrangement. Opposite is the arched, carved, heavy wooden bed dominating the room, with matching bedside tables. There is no armoire entertainment cabinet, as the flat-screen hangs over the fireplace, easily viewed from the bed. A low dressing table completes the bed suite. An arched doorway leads to the immense attaching bath and walk-in closet.

For now, it's only the bedroom he sees. Too soon for the other reveal. A lady's bed is one thing. Her closet and bath are altogether another. These are areas of intimate mystery, to be viewed only when the occasion and relationship are right. Not before.

Sam's silence troubles me.

"Too much?" I nibble on a thumbnail, a habit I've sworn off since puberty, with the striking realization that boys wouldn't be a problem.

They never looked at me anyway. Soon after, I swore off indoor garden modeling—posing as a wallflower—and began focusing on those too-long-neglected, overlooked plants and flowers that attempted to grow outside in the sunshine and shade of real life. They, like me, seem willing, yearning, struggling to flourish if only given the tiniest bit of TLC.

Tugging my hand from my mouth, replacing my lips with those of his own, Sam slowly shakes his head. Slowly, ever so slowly—like the man in my dreams who has found his way home, weary and worn, filled with elation after years traversing the world, battling heaven and hell, tide and mountain, to return to my loving embrace and the space between my thighs—Sam turns to me, sinking to his knees. A man. This man. Sam. Kneeling before me. Me. *Me.* ME.

Sam is right. I do need him. Only him.

Tears spring forth, flowing freely down my cheeks. Sam encircles my hips and waist with his strong, solid arms. Burrowing his face into my belly and loins, he inhales deeply, rolling his face around from cheek to cheek, as if testing all the comfort options to be had pressed to my middle, pillowy softness. Leaving me unsure of how to proceed.

I know what I've dreamed of doing.

Fingers, tentative at first, find their way to his riot of wavy and curly hair. Combing my fingers through that midnight cascade of silk, I stroke and massage to my heart's content. A contented smile peeks out. Indulgence seems to be the name of this course. I lean forward, my nose burrowing into a length of his hair, retreating with the lingering aroma of Sam. Lips replace the nose. Eyes close.

While my hands are busy exploring, so, too, are Sam's. Loosening his grip, he soothes his hands liberally over the back of my frame. Back, hips, legs, these he explores with the flats of his fingers, the backs of his hands, and, at times, his nails. It's when he reaches my backside that his touch changes.

Molding, memorizing my posterior flesh is seemingly the goal. My clothing, an impediment. Sam's hands find their way under my winter-layered barriers, meant to conceal and hide all. Sam is intent on revealing all, feeling his way around to accomplish this feat down to the source, the core and crust of what is me in the flesh.

Skin on skin makes me gasp. Naked lips on naked flesh makes me jump. Sam raises his head. His intent is detecting the true meaning of my response. "Again, or no more?"

"More. Then again, and more yet again."

My words please him. Like air popcorn popping, Sam is on his feet. We're in each other's arms. Limbs entwine. We're flinging and tossing clothing, heedless of where it may land. Not even the crashing of a lamp gives us pause. It only sets us to laughing, spurring more intense and frantic speed to rid each other and ourselves of that which impedes.

While I'm reaching for my bra, Sam flings out a hand to stay my move. "No. Don't."

My questioning eyes search his face. Has he finally come to his senses?

Realizing that his words have taken my brain down a different path, heading for the wasteland called vulnerability, he entreats, "Daria, let me. If you please, allow *me*. It has always been my dream to do this."

"What, this?" I ask, indicating the bit of cotton and lace.

Adam's apple bobbing, Sam swallows and nods. Licks his lips. I watch, mesmerized, as those edges of that divine aperture form his words. "Will you allow it, sweet Daria?"

"Yes."

With a grace surprising to myself, I lower my arms. Before him I stand.

Confusion. Fear. These emotions and others war with my brain and my heart when Sam makes no move.

"Having second thoughts?" I ask, peering up at him. My lower lip is once more pinched by a few of my gnawing teeth.

An are-you-kidding-me look settles on his face. "I see I shall have to be patient…"

A sudden idea takes root, brightening his eyes. Extending a hand, he beckons me. Gently, he pulls me to stand before him, my back to his front. Intimately, Sam presses against me. He has us facing the hanging antique, full-length mirror.

"See this? Us? You? This, and what lies within, has always attracted me. Your home, garden…this," he purrs, sweeping the length of me, "say who you are. Seemingly, you seek to project the appearance of normalcy, when in fact you are not. Never will be, and my bet is that you never have been…average."

I blink rapidly, unsure of what matter of batter is being creamed. His emotional whipping, emotional custard in the making, isn't at an end.

"It's all veneer you project." He's killing me softly. "Designed to fool and conceal what truly lies beneath and within."

Phoenix peeking tentatively through ash and flame. Oh, how she longs to rise and soar.

"Wh-what is that? What do you think I harbor and hide within?" Texas-sized chocolate-pecan-caramel turtles. Is this a tequila sun on the rise?

"Passion. Richness, solid and deep. Umami—savory, as in smoked BBQ, rich dark chocolate, or sipping port on a cold winter's night before a roaring fire. Piquant zest that leaves a mouthwatering tang in its wake. I've not begun to uncover the richness of the flavor that is Daria. You *will* come to explain why it is you work so hard to conceal. But now…now I want to treat myself to my first full tasting of Daria."

Phoenix rising.

"Allow me? Allow us? Allow yourself?"

"Yes. Be my guest. Truly, it shall be my pleasure, and hope-fully"—Sam raises a brow at the last—"yours."

Deep groaning of something too long pent up finally freed. "Long have I wanted to stand where I do now. Daria, you are a feast for my eyes. My heart likes what it sees. More and more, you are a feast for all of my senses. Only you can sate my long-held desires. Fill my soul."

Can such words be believed? Words spoken about and to me? My Willy Wonka world is real.

My parting lips vent shuddering breaths. Deep color stains my cheeks, adding to the look of being tipsy on the wine of possi-bilities, of hope, of rapture that matches the dewy wetness of my eyes. Silently, I watch with trembling breath, through quivering lips, as his hands, resting upon my shoulders, smooth down my arms, taking with them the straps of my burgundy-lace bra. Back clasp undone. Sam pulls down and then away that last thread of inhibi-tion, baring in abundance all there is to his gaze. Gone is the bit of seductively supportive fabric meant to reveal-conceal. Tantalized, Sam's eyes and fingers explore what and where few have gone be-fore. Few have desired and fewer invited to view beneath the lay-ers of clothing what modesty dictates should conceal and conceal further still.

With wondrous eyes looking through the looking glass, we each watch the other's wondering and wandering eyes as we take our fill, for now. Darker-toned, baked-to-perfection, sun-kissed golden arms reach around me as hands reach further still to cap-ture and uplift pale, raspberry-tipped mountains of smooth but-termilk breasts.

Work-roughened hands are employed as tools. They begin a gentle exploration, becoming bolder, rougher, tempering as they study just how to please and gain pleasure.

"Beautiful," he utters.

A single tear rolls down my cheek.

Closing my eyes, I tilt my head, granting and inviting him access to my neck. Lips now add to the mix of our carnal delight of a sexual appetizer. If this is the bread-and-spread starter portion of the meal, I am more than ready for the next serving. Salad and soup me. As if on cue, Sam senses the need for more.

Tootsie-rolling me around in his arms, he pulls me to stand pressed front to front. Exploring hands continue their voyage of discovery along my mirror-reflected hams.

"See these full moons?" Sam asks a bit breathlessly as he watches his hands surveying via braille method the craters and curves that make up that mass. I dare a peek over my shoulder at that wonder, wondering just what it is that he finds so…wondrous.

"Like all forces of gravity, they were the first to pull me into your orbit. This is the first part of you I ever saw."

Momentum interruptus. *Huh?*

"When I first viewed the property," he says, gesturing head toward his home. "Standing on the back deck, surveying the yard and all that lay beyond, I spied this." A hand caresses the entire expanse of exposed skin. "And you. Wearing cutoff jean shorts, baggy, torn, and dirty, what should have been a white tee falling off one shoulder, and a large beach hat, barefoot, kneeling on the ground, bent over one of your precious plants. You were crooning to the thing. You. Your honey buns. Your voice…Knew then what I wanted. No remorse. Stepping beyond the privet hedge blocking the public to the private side of your house and yard is like stepping into an alternate universe."

"You wanted, still want, an alternate reality?"

"Are you daft, woman?" He pushes me back to peer into another set of questioning, wondering orbs. "It's more than just the world *you* created and the truth of that *real* world that I wanted… want. I crave the goddess. The one who created all that lays before me and lays hidden beneath and within."

Said goddess jumps the man, catapulting him to land with his back on the bed, with me his blanket. Frantic hands rid each other of any and all remaining coverings, mindless of the renting of cloth. Naked at last. Feasting ensues. Fingers, lips, tongues the tools of our frenzy feeding. Gouda, I'm starved.

Sam rolls us, placing me on my back so that all I see is him. A devilish gleam shines from his wickedly enthralling eyes, making them more so.

"Can I sample—nibble and lick—your pie?"

"What? Not afraid it's gone beyond its expiration date?"

"Daria," he says in a warning tone, "no more of that. Bite your tongue for now; we'll work on ridding you of that garbage, that bitter baggage you seem reluctant to let go. Pain is like pus, it must be released, expressed fully to rid it completely so it doesn't poison the soul, the body. It shouldn't be hoarded."

Eew. Pimple popping, emotional or dermatological, is not what I wish to indulge in right now.

"But coming from a man, trust me when I say, your pie is," he says dramatically, sniffing and savoring the air, "fresh." Shimmying down my length, he continues, "And incredibly warm and"—head-in-the-oven muffled voice, a flicking of tongue—"incredibly moist. As for the taste…" Slurping, sipping, savoring. "Yummy." He goes to town, chowing down in his need to give and gain pleasure.

Phoenix with spread wings, soaring.

Lying back, I spread my shanks wider. "Have at it, all that you want. There's lots."

I yelp as his hand comes in sharp contact with the edge of one of the full moons he enjoys. Too far into this honey-pot quaffing, it takes no time bringing me to that final summit on Candy Mountain. The phoenix yells out a joyful *kiyee.*

"Sam." Orgasmic Skittles wash over me in colorful dots of bliss.

"Entrée time. Or is this the dessert?" he teases, or does he?

He's smiling while slip-sliding up my still-quivering form, which glistens from passion's dew, coating my bliss-flushed and heated flesh. Finding the right oven for his beefy Frank Swellington, he skewers me, filling me with his Ball Park–sized, hanging-beyond-the-bun frankfurter.

"First penetration of the pie requires a moment of reverent stillness," he says, breathlessly teasing me as much as his fully rooted probe. I press my hands firmly to his two golden buns, arching my hips, signaling permission to begin moving. He does.

Easy, slow, small moves at first. Experimenting with variants, he picks the one recipe for the situation at hand. Saving languid for later, he selects a tried-and-true oldie but goodie, explaining, "Not sure how long I can last before I fill you with my cream."

My response is turning my head and licking the trickle of salty sweat rolling down the side of his face. Gasping and groaning as he buries his face in the side of my neck, Sam's hips pick up a pounding rhythm. KitchenAid on or near maximum speed. Faster and harder he churns the crock. Wider I spread my legs, hooking my ankles around the backs of his thighs. Gruntings signal his approaching completion. Reaching down, Sam hoists up one of my legs, hooking it in the crook of his arm, widening me still. Another variation. I like that.

We come together.

Perfect timing.

Chapter 8

Daria

Blotting my lips once again, trying to not survey myself in the mirror while surveying myself in the mirror, I complete the last touches of my personal prep before heading out the door to Mom and Dad's.

Since this was dinner at my folks' place, I selected to upgrade my attire. No workout gear tonight. Casual it is, so casual I will be. Then, thinking of all that Sam said before, during, and after...I decide on going a bit bolder than my parents are used to seeing. I select black leggings, pairing them with a white, long-sleeved, mock turtleneck tunic, topped with a royal-purple ruana, belted. Knee-length boots in royal-purple leather finish it off, along with large, dangling, gaily decorated sugar cookie earrings. Fun.

Mascara and twenty-four-hour stay-on lipstick is all the makeup I wear. With my hair brushed and gleaming, I leave it hanging down, tucking a hair elastic in my pocket for if and when needed.

"Hmm." Critical assessment time. "Thumbs-up? Thumbs-down? Sideways?" I ask the plus-sized woman in the mirror. "Not bad, all in all." Hello to my start of showing Daria Downer the door and welcoming in Daria Delight. One of the lasting things to come out of that…whatever it was…thingy with Sam.

The sex—great. Two days after our lingering, lip-clinging goodbye-for-now-but-I-really-need-to-shower-and-sleep kiss, I'm still sore in selective spots. Pausing to rest and recharge, we went at it again and again. And again. I learned that something else nice about working from home as well as your hot neighbor with benefits, beyond a request for a cup of sugar, or sex, is the daylong, extending-into-nighttime nooky.

The only reason for our hiatus—work and family obligations. In order to have a successful at-home career, one has to actually work. At home. Sam had clients to meet and scheduled installs and inspections awaiting him. I had my editing jobs and my blog. There was also the novel currently under final revision.

Then there was family. *Ugh.*

"When can we see each other again?" Sam's question had me momentarily stilling, searching my brain for the hook. He continued, kissing and licking the curve of my shoulder, "I don't want you thinking that I'm an easy lay, but babe, me and…"

"Frank Beef Swellington? The footlong Coke can living downstairs?" I teased, flicking my appreciative gaze to what was now sleeping behind two layers of cotton. Twinkling eyes accompanied by a mock shocked expression met my words. "Not that I'm complaining," I hastily amended.

"Only a foot long, huh? Hah, yeah, him…Don't want to go away feeling cheap and used. I want to know that you value me—us, not just for *his* uplifting personality and my considerable finesse in wielding his meaty might." He gave a cute, cheeky grin, leaving me gooey, again.

"Girl's got to have her fun collecting her boy toys…"

"What does your calendar look like?" he asks. "Got a family thing this Saturday…"

"Me too!" I say, scratching that day off the mental calendar.

"That leaves us two…"

"Hey, ho there, I'm not a pencil-me-in call girl." I found myself caught between wanting to laugh and being pissed. "Not so sure I want to be considered a 'sure thing' until this…thing we've got going—and off to a good start, by the way—is better defined."

"So what are you saying?" Sam queried.

"Penciling you in makes me feel cheap, as if this is a revenue source…"

"Making me—"

I cut him off. "Another customer. And bub, that just ain't my style."

Faster than a hot knife through butter, I was flat on my back, with Sam's nose pressed deeply into my love muffin. Inhaling deep, muffling…Or was that a bit of a nibble I detected?

"All I smell here is me and you." Lifting head from my crotch, he said, "Better smell nobody else down here."

Was he warning or just playing?

"Well, butter my butt and call me a biscuit." I batted my eyes coyly. "Darling, until you put a ring on it or we agree to exclusivity, you're just gonna have to take your chances," I said, saucily dishing back.

In softer yet serious tones, a swipe of a swat on his arm, then cradling his face, I add, "Hey, I know this is sudden, sort of a building boil that was bound to pop." I cringe at the mental picture. "Bad metaphor, but you get my meaning. I know you have responsibilities and obligations. Well, news flash, so do I."

We move to sitting positions. "Just come over when you can,

and I'll do the same. If we're too busy to be interrupted, then we'll have no hard feelings and keep trying until we find a way to make it all gel. Okay?"

Since then our days have been left for working, the evenings and nights reserved for us. I even allowed him into those sacred inner sanctums within a woman's boudoir. Well, I couldn't make the man hold his pee or use the guest bathroom after all we'd seen and done with one another. Sam taking care of his business required passing through the gateway into another realm—my walk-in closet and farther, into my holy of holies—my private en suite bathroom.

"Through that door you'll find the throne room," I informed Sam when I saw the desperate need flash in his eyes that he wouldn't mention. I recognized it the moment I saw it. The same look my nephews get when they need to tinkle and don't want to ask where it is or stop what they're doing.

A stone-accented, arched doorway leads into a short hallway with a stone-covered, barrel-vaulted ceiling. Motion-activated lights illuminated the floor, causing the hurrying, pitter-patter shuffling of Sam's feet to falter. I smiled a crooked smile when I heard him mutter, "Cool."

I mentally counted his imagined steps before following in pursuit. Having no desire to witness him evacuating his bladder, I was, however, keenly interested in his reaction to what he would be encountering before that event, provided what he saw didn't make him piss prematurely and in the wrong area. Then I'd be pissed and would make him do the cleanup.

Low lighting began glowing seconds before Sam exclaimed, "Holy mo…" Mumblings continued, as did the pitter-patter shuffling, stopping once again to be replaced by the distinct sound of fountaining lemonade.

"Aww," Sam exclaimed, making concealing my cheesy grin impossible. The almost silent *whoosh* of the toilet sounded from behind its discreet enclosure. I designed most of my bathing area out in the open. The toilet, however, is a private matter and should be more privately framed, even in the privacy of a private and exclusive room.

My intrepid neighbor now turned lover didn't immediately return. I could hear him as he furthered his expedition, exploring the space. The motion-sensitive floor lighting softly illuminated his steps. He knew I was watching.

"Daria, no need to remain hidden in the shadows." He beckoned me with an outstretched arm and twiddling, curling, come-hither fingers, magic wanding me to approach. Under the spell, his spell, I did.

"This another one of the modifications you alluded to earlier?"

"Uhm-hmm. Like my bathroom?" My saucy smile was suppressed unsuccessfully.

"This, woman," he said, gesturing to the whole of the room, "is no bathroom. It's a frigging magnificent Roman caldarium." I love a man who knows his history. "A Tuscan—sensing an aesthetic theme here—bathing chamber complete with"—he dipped a toe into the central feature, a built-in, walk-in, heated spa-pool bathtub—"elevated fountain fonts for sinks, hidden niches for personal supply items, mosaic and tile flooring, barrel-vaulted ceiling, and heated bathing pool." He pulled me behind him, and we stepped down into the circular bath, sinking into the warm waters of the pool. Sam startled with amazement as underwater lights illuminated the depths.

Before submerging, I pressed a button starting the suck and flow of the water through the Tuscan bronze waterfall faucet. "Not big enough to do laps, but large enough to float, soak, and stationary swim." I sighed with dreamy contentment. "I've dreamed of such a place since visiting Roman and Turkish baths while traveling. The rich, darker tones of the Tuscan style appeal to me a bit more than the creams and whites of Grecian and Turkish baths."

"When was this? The traveling," he asked.

"With my aunt Alphia. When I reached a certain age, she took me as her travel companion on most of her trips."

"I see a separate walk-in shower…"

"For cleansing. This is for…"

"Luxuriating," he murmured as he wrapped his arms around me from behind. By the time we emerged from the water, our skin was pruny as pickles.

While drying off, Sam said, "We are *never* showing my mother this closet." He emphasized his words with a shake of his head.

We both were now encased in plush Turkish cotton robes. Our bath play having ended, Sam was feeling a bit more exploratory. Sex seemed to energize him.

"How come?" I asked, running a finger up and down my wrinkling nose. Sam shooed my finger and hand away, plopping a kiss just there.

"Pops won't ever speak to me again. Mom will have him converting the spare into her royal regina room, a diva den designed to house her female fripperies and fashion," he explained as he waltzed around the space. Gesturing above his head, he asked, "A crystal chandelier? And what have we here? Wherever did you find this antique circular boudoir settee? Looks like it came out of some French courtesan's private bedchamber."

Shrugging, I felt my blush burning as it intensified. "I wanted a completely feminine room. Not as cavity-inducing as it could be, which is why I went with cream, brushed-burnished gold, and crystal with a touch of purple, not candy pink."

"And this is what you designed for your clothing and fashion accessories." Nonchalantly flicking the few hanging garments with a finger, he mused, "All this space and barely filled."

"Well, the organization of my garments allows me to critically review what I've got and what I need. I try to keep it at that. It's not like I need tons anyway…" He still hasn't seen my shopping mall of a closet downstairs. Yo-yo dieting and the constant gain and loss of significant weight has resulted in the overaccumulation of clothing, mostly clothing that no longer fits. I've relegated those items in an organized fashion downstairs. I do my shopping from there first.

Sam held up a warning finger. His frown was quickly replaced with the leering grin of a wicked, deviant devil. "Good choice, love. I rather prefer you bare."

Frothy foam topping. Was this guy for real?

"Seeing all this makes me wonder what your office is like. Seeing your kitchen, where your magic is brewed, and your bed and bath, where heaven is to be had, now this…What did your mom say when she first saw it?"

The question had me flinching, a movement that did not escape his notice. Tilting his head, he remarked, "She's not seen it." Statement, not question.

I nodded.

Silently, he approached, gathering me to him. He pressed my head to his breast and shoulder, petting my damp hair. "Why? How long have you lived here?"

"Three years," I admitted in a petulant whisper.

"Thr…and she's never been here? Inside? Daria…"

"Mom keeps a busy schedule…"

"Try again."

"Timing was never right, or something unexpected always

comes up. Like on the day of my open house when I'd finally moved in. I invited family and a few close friends over for the grand reveal and a finger meal."

"And…"

"Mom ended up a no-show, saying she was sick. That's okay, I mean, it's not like anyone really showed anyway." I shrugged in the safety of his hold. *Damn that escaping tear, and that one too.* Next thing I knew, I was blubbering like a baby.

When my tears finally dried, Sam pushed me away, yet he maintained contact, with his hands keeping hold of my arms.

Peering into my eyes, he asked, "What? Nobody came?" Incredulousness colored his face, which was morphing through too many emotions for me to keep track. I turned away, nodding, and shrugged, not wanting the waterworks to begin all over again. A sore subject.

"Tell me." Soft words whispering into my ear compelled me as Sam cupped my shoulders, pulling me back into the solid reality of his frame. I did.

"Dad came for a brief time. He examined and praised all there was to see. I prepared him a takeaway food box for him and Mom." Breaking free of his hold, I turned and walked a few steps away and curled my arms around myself. "I'd laid out a grazing feast for fifty. Only ten showed, briefly."

"Let me guess. Clarise and Tabitha, with their men in tow…"

I nodded. "I hadn't even invited them," I confessed, a blush staining my cheeks.

"They crashed your party?" He guffaws. "The Meadows?"

Again, I nod.

"Siblings? I assume you aren't an only child."

"Victoria, my younger, prettier, skinnier"—waving and swirling of the hand—"everything-er sister, didn't last any longer than it took to walk the length of the house. After casing the place, she marched right up to me after snagging a flute of bubbly and tossed the contents in my face before stomping out the door. One brother, Tom, the oldest, stayed a bit longer, lecturing about how my modifications and aesthetics weren't good for the resale value. Braden, my other brother, loved the place and wanted to stay, but he had come with Victoria, sooo…The others didn't linger. Couldn't blame them."

"Stop it, Daria. You have a right to be hurt, to be angry. But that last comment is way out of line. Such self-disparaging indirect and direct comments will cease. Now. A nonnegotiable term of our relationship. But back to the other topic…your family. Why weren't they crowing your success? This place…*You* should be proud, regardless of their behavior, of what *you've* accomplished."

"Oh, I think they are each secretly proud. I think they love me. Have to believe that, but there are things and dynamics that you don't understand…" So I filled in a few blanks.

He hadn't been scared off yet. A true test regarding whether a new relationship has staying power is if the other will stay when they get the lowdown of one's family.

"My family isn't perfect. Doubt there really is such a thing. Warts and all, I still love them. Even when their good intentions hurt."

"What did you do with the food?"

That gets me laughing a bit.

"Go-boxes. Told them the lie that it was from an exclusive caterer called *For the Love of Food*, drove some over to Mr. James's, you know Cyrus, as I heard his wife was ailing. Took the rest to a homeless shelter."

"That's it?"

"Mom did say something curious when she phoned the other day."

"Yeah?"

"Said that she was aware I wasn't getting out much. Wasn't sure if it was Momdar in play or some cryptic remark that she's been having me surveilled..."

"Yeah, I've experienced the Momdar phenomenon more than once. Can be like the eye of Mordor." He shuddered for effect. "Maybe she has a friend in the area..."

We both shook our heads in the midst of the conundrum.

"Well, at least it shows she cares," Sam offered. "She has a strange way of showing it, but maybe she feels *she's* the failure."

My eyes opened wide, physically and metaphorically. "Mom? Failure? At what?" I made scoffing noises of disbelief mixed with a bit of confusion.

"Failure as a mom. Fear that it wasn't her that guided you to this moment."

"So, jealousy, then..." I snorted in derision. "As to the other... I'll need more time, a lot more time to process it, but she is part of why I am what I am..."

Sam holds up a finger. "Let me guess. You're the firstborn girl." He nailed it in one. Only my brother Tom is older.

"And as such you became a surrogate parent to your other siblings." Taking in the expression on my face, he added, "Hey, you aren't the only one with their own kind of magic powers." I uplifted a brow at his words. "Babe, you are a garden goddess, a food fairy, and a kitchen witch. In the bedroom..." His lips captured mine in a deepening kiss that deepened our arousal even further.

"As I was saying..." He cleared his throat. "As the eldest..." Seems Sam was the eldest in his family too. Birth order theories are seemingly correct.

"In my case," I decided fair play dictated I share, "Mom was young, ambitious. Tom did preschool and was picked up by grandparents. Mom didn't want to give up her career just yet. Aunt Alphia was the one to raise me, until I was old enough to stay at home and tend the other two."

"And you were roped into raising them. To see to their needs and wants before your own. So when good ole—"

"Fat, unmarried, overlooked and unappreciated by most, but the most wonderful person ever."

"—Aunt Alphia rewarded the one most deserving, the others allowed their demons to appear. And, I imagine, in spades," he concluded.

Yeah, some cousins and other extended family members haven't spoken to me since.

"Hindsight being what it is, I probably shouldn't have even attempted the open house. They must have thought I was bragging. You know, rubbing their noses in it," I said, wrinkling mine.

"Agreed. Besides, truth being so candidly displayed of the proverbial reaping of one's reward or being paid what one's due must have really hit home."

"Hmmm. Every moment I spent in Aunt Alphia's company was sheer joy. Given a choice, I'd choose Auntie A over Mom. I love Mom, but she can be…harsh and overly critical. Her tongue is a weapon she uses with and without thought. Not so with Auntie A. She clucked and soothed. Aunt Alphia I loved. Still do. And she loved every stitch of me, warts and all. She made me feel good, normal. Worthy. Fact is, I don't think anyone had a clue just what she had accumulated or how she acquired her comfortable living," I shared. "So as the dutiful eldest daughter, I am obligated to have dinner with my parents Saturday. Can't get out of it now. I've promised to bring too much already. Still can't deny them or say no. Especially when Mom's doing the asking and demanding."

Yeah, the come-for-dinner invite has turned into a "since you're coming, why not bring the dinner too?" event. She's employed the cooking services of *For the Love of Food*. Something she's been crowing about to her friends. I'm meant to pick up and deliver.

"And so it is with me. And as the children we are, we shall abide this parental-dictated request. Later we shall have our own feast," Sam said.

Sam parted my robe as I twined my arms around his neck. Dipping his head, he proceeded to lick his way from my left nipple up, following the contours of my body before settling on my lips.

The memory of what transpired from there puts a nice stain on my cheeks, making the need for blush unnecessary. With a last pop of my lips to set my lipstick and a last look in the mirror, I heave a deep sigh. The car is loaded. Nothing left to do. No more excuses to delay the inevitable. It is time to head over to Mom and Dad's. I begin the countdown until I could next lay eyes and more on Sam and headed out the door.

Chapter 9

Sam

"Why is the minivan out in the drive with the engine running?" I ask, throwing out the question to those in the living room.

All I get are owl eyes.

"Well, Son," Dad finally begins replying. He adjusts his easy-boy recliner, making the leather creak before pulling out the toothpick stuck between his lips, his tool for breaking his smoking habit. "That's what you do when warming up the car. Not safe to do it in the garage," Dad explains as he would to my younger sister.

Said sister rolls her eyes. "No, Daaad, Sam wants to know why it's being warmed up," she translates.

Mom walks into the room. "Because we're going over to my friend Rachel's house for dinner. Change of plans. She invited, and when I was politely declining, giving her my reasons, she waved them off, saying to bring the lot of you," she informs me while fastening an earring in place. Momdar. "One less meal for me to make and clean up." Luke pumps his fist, not in sight of Mom, or so he thinks. "Friends and family to surround myself with...No brainer," Mom says, flopping her arms as if she were still a teenager, making everyone chuckle and giggle indulgently.

"What am I to do with my food offering?" I ask, still holding up the carefully packed, layered box of appetizer fare that Daria so sweetly and quickly assembled when I told her of my plight. Scorecards included.

"Bring with. From what I gather, there will be plenty of mouths to feed," Mom says, patting my cheek before herding the rest toward donning their coats before heading out the door.

Whipping around with the mom finger pointing at me, causing me to fling up one hand in surrender while bobbling the box dangerously with the other, she pointedly instructs, "Oh, and Sam, be nice. I expect you to be on your best behavior."

Mouthing, "What, me?" while pointing my finger at myself, an action Mom chooses to ignore. So I point my finger at each of my siblings, raising a knowing brow in turn. I get scoffs and suppressed giggles in return.

"When Rachel learned that you've been away and have only recently returned to the bosom of your family"—her words elicit snickers from my younger siblings, which has her tossing them mom warnings without losing stride or train of thought—"Rachel seemed keen on having you join us."

"Got two"—holding up fingers—"unmarried daughters," Dad says with a straight face.

"Mooom," I begin in a voice filled with aggravation, "I have no desire for the matchmaking machinations you or your *dear friends* try foisting on me. Besides, I've met someone already. I'm taken."

Domino effect. Mom's forward motion abruptly halts, causing all in her wake to plow into one another to keep from toppling into her. Nimble Dad sidesteps, keeping his full momentum striding forward, reaching the van first. Winner. Clever or coward?

Quickly, like they are at a tennis match, my siblings' heads volley between Mom and myself. Interested parties are all glued to the ensuing play-by-play. Front row and center. With large, blinking eyes and a comical face, a mixture of disbelief and aggravation, Mom seeks more information.

"What do you mean?" The sides of her nostrils are winging with the near-frantic puffing of her breathing as the she-beast sniffs for any and all signs that her son is lying.

"He's met a girl, Mom," Matthew pipes in, taking one step forward and two back when Mom's eyes swing to him.

"And he loooves her." Lucy giggles.

Luke playfully rubs his hand down her face to quit her smirking tee-heeing. What can I say? Lucy is the baby at the ripe old age of fourteen.

"And he's had sex with her," Luke supplies dryly with a devilish glint in his eyes.

Mom's gasping outrage reaches sonic decibels at being informed that *her* children indulge in such naughty and wanton behavior. As if she hasn't and doesn't.

I clamp down tight on my brain, hoping such images won't take root in my head.

Taking a deep breath, glancing at her watch, and giving up a bit of a grunt, Mother Goose continues leading her goslings to the warm and waiting vehicle. "Is it true?" she asks over her shoulder.

"Yes."

"Yes to what?" she demands.

Sighing dramatically. "Yes to meeting a woman, a real one. Yes to loving her. Yes to having...having"—I place my hands over Lucy's ears—"sex with her. Many times, with plans for more to come on that score." I release Lucy's head amid her giggles. The brat has heard every word and is letting me know it. Imp.

"How long have you known this...this..."

"Wonderfully fantastic, creative, successful, passionate—"

"Smoochable," Lucy adds, pursing her lips and adding sound effects.

"Sensual," Luke throws in. "Hubba-hubba."

"Totally bonkers," Matthew offers. We all turn to him. "Both Sam and the chick," he clarifies.

"—Beautiful and loving woman?" I supply, crooking a brow, one that mirrors Mom's own. "Any lesser or negative description would be false. And if uttered by you, unacceptable and uncalled for, not to mention unkind and not of the mettle and honor of the heart of the woman that I call Mother." My piercing gaze is wavering, so I look down at my nails and rub them against my woolen peacoat before casually inspecting them. "Particularly if said mother doesn't want the neighbors witnessing said grown son having a throw down here and now and said son storming off until said mother has apologized profusely and earnestly." I raise a brow in expectation.

Line in the sand drawn.

All wait in anticipation.

Dad has even rolled down the car window.

One Mississippi. Two Mississippi.

"Quite right. Not the sort of thing a dignified person would do." Mom harrumphs. "Unless said mother is correct and said young lady is unworthy of said mother's son. Such as an overstepping floozy, tramp, or worse."

"Which she is *not*," I say in a hard, sharp voice. "She is truly remarkable, Mom. She has her own business—two of them, actually. Both quite successful. Her garden puts yours to shame, as do her culinary skills." Mom is narrowing her eyes, dangerously so. "Her custom-built home she designed is worthy of being in *Architectural Digest*. We'll have you all over for dinner at her place soon, and you'll see for yourselves." I'm hoping I can convince Daria of this now that I have committed us.

"Besides, Lucy's right." A beaming and victorious smile comes from that one. "I love her."

"Well, what am I to tell Rachel?"

"Try telling her the truth?" Dad suggests, tossing me a supportive look in the rearview mirror.

"That could work," Mom muses as she fastens her seat belt, then crosses her arms as if I've just disappointed her. Certainly dashed some plans she's been cooking up. Good.

"Are we bringing anything more than my contribution to tonight's nonmatchmaking event?" I ask, trying to change the topic.

"It's packed in the back. We're bringing rolls and dessert," Mom says, a bit glum.

"What sort of dessert?"

"Spice cake with real whipped-cream icing, French-style apple pie, strawberry-rhubarb crumble, and brownies. All made from scratch, including the rolls."

All things I had smelled coming from Daria's kitchen. Coincidence?

"Gosh, Mom, when did you learn to bake?" Wrong words. I know it the moment they slide off my tongue. Glancing at the rearview mirror, I see Dad's pitying look. A glance at Lucy has her drawing a finger across her throat. I gulp.

Whirling around, hands on her hips, Mom demands, "And what is that supposed to mean?"

"Though your culinary talents are extreme—"

"—ly bad, and ER-requiring," Luke stage whispers.

"Are extreme and well known," I continue, glaring at my siblings, "baking is a talent you've left for others so their skills may grow and shine." Matthew hands over his unused handkerchief, which I use to blot my brow. His nod and slight pursing lips suggest I may have played this one well. My hand slightly trembles. Still too early to say with certainty.

"Well. Seeing that I had so many additional mouths to fill, I thought it best to get a real professional to assist," Mom says, somewhat mollified.

"Local caterer," Luke supplies in a low tone. "Plump chick with a great shape, curves in all the right places, and fabulous hair. Pretty." He makes serpentine, hourglass movements with his hands, emphasizing bust and hip curves.

"When last at the salon—" Mom dabs at her recently coiffed hairdo.

"Beautiful," Pop murmurs to her, casting her hungry eyes, to Mom's delight. He leans over to plant a kiss on her cheek. As the eldest son, I dutifully cover Lucy's eyes, then her mouth to prevent any verbal response. The plopping of a gooey tongue in the center of my palm has me quickly retracting it, reaching back a seat, and wiping it on Luke's shoulder.

"—I got the number of this *exclusive* caterer. Having tasted some of their culinary creations, I *just had* to have them." She swivels her head around like Linda Blair in *The Exorcist*, causing me and my smarter siblings to move as far back in our seats as possible. We keep the presence of mind to not cross ourselves fast and furiously, though Luke holds up Lucy's silver Celtic cross necklace charm, shielding himself with her body as he sits behind her. Yeah, as if that will really save us.

"I think I just made holy water," Matthew discloses as he squirms in his seat.

"Eew." We all shift, peering down at our feet, fearing he wasn't fooling.

"Don't. Say. A word," the demon possessing my mom speaks from her body.

A silent chorus of head-shakings, noddings, and zipping-lip motions accompanied by fear-widened eyes follows.

"Dare you to douse the demon with your holy water," I whisper to Matthew, gaining appreciative chuckles, snorts, and muffled giggles.

Blessedly, the ride is short. There's a slight exiting chaos as boxes are handed off for each to carry. Clustered together, we move up the long, winding walk to the front door.

"Caterer?" I venture, frowning at the are-you-crazy looks from my siblings. I return with a shoulder move and mouthing a silent, "What?"

"Exclusive," Mom affirms. "Considered a real boon if anyone gets them to agree to a job."

"If it's sooo exclusive, how did you manage to snag them?"

Dad bops the back of my head.

Yeah, I deserved that one. Apologetic look to Mom. First, she gives me the mom-glare, then the twinkling eyes. All is forgiven. But she can be sneaky.

"I called the number I was given. You can only reach them by phone. No shop. No address. All so mysterious. I placed my order, and a person delivered it earlier today."

Hmmm.

"Got a name for this phantom foodie?"

"Fabulous website that is *all the rage* called *For the Love of Food*."

Say what?

"Now, shush, I hear someone coming."

The door opens. Greeting us is a slender, pretty blonde with brown eyes. The devil is in her eyes and aimed at me.

Sighing, I think, *Let the letdown begin.*

■ ■ ■

Daria

"You're late!" Mom hisses as I enter through the garage. "Whatever *are* you wearing?"

"Well, hello to you too," I snark as I stumble over the threshold, arms full of a heavy box overly laden with portions of tonight's meal.

That has Mom stopping in midstride and midpush, throwing me off balance even more.

"Attitude, Daria. I haven't the time or patience to deal with it," she snaps back.

Uhm-kay.

"You're late! I have a house *full* of people who've come for dinner, and dinner...Not only is not ready—it. Isn't. Here." Deep breaths.

Hmmm. I'm starting to smell a scheming rat. Let's test this theory.

"What's the big deal? It's just family, Mom. Besides, *you* invited *me*. The question is, in what capacity? Since I also brought the meal. Was I hoodwinked into doing so—"

"How hard can it be? I order it. You pick it up and transport it."

Grrr. "There is the gathering of the ingredients and the actual making of the food, you know. You all could have just come to my place. Sure would have been easier for me. In fact, if being here now is suuuch a problem, I can rectify that instantly." Moving back toward the door, I say, "I'll simply go home."

"No! Daria!" Closing her eyes, she takes more deep breaths, sliding into a more dignified and demure veneer before my very eyes.

"Mom, while you're thinking up a response...Time is of the essence. This box is rather heavy, and I either need to set it down quickly or risk ruining it all by dropping it where we stand. And that mess I will not be cleaning." I dramatically increase the trembling of my arms, which results in the dishes inside clanking ominously. "Don't know how much longer I can hold it." Daughter and mother alpha-glare until daughter pretends to drop the box.

"Okay, okay," Mom concedes, dragging me farther into the kitchen, where I plop the box down in the nick of time.

"There's more in the car..."

"Well, go get it." Mom impatiently sweeps her hand.

Angrily blinking my eyes and pursing my lips, I place my hands on my hips. "Mom. What gives? Besides, I can't and won't do it all by myself. This needs to be unpacked and other items brought in. Your kitchen isn't even prepped," I add with a sweep of my hand.

Growling and tossing me a feral glare, she stomps off, muttering, "I'll get your brother."

This implies both tons and nothing, all at the same time. Without shucking my coat, I turn on the oven and a few burners I'll be needing before unpacking the box.

Stomping precedes voice. "Hey, sis, got a task needing doing?" Braden enters, pausing to kiss me on the cheek.

"Where's Tom, Katie, and the kids? Victoria?"

His head gestures toward the common room. Hmmm.

"Yeah, got more in the car. Lemon meringue. I sure can use the help. Can also use a bit of information and explanations too," I say to his retreating form.

"What'dya bring?" Braden, ever the eager eater, asks, practically dancing from foot to foot in his enthusiasm. He never ceases to make me laugh.

"Well, we've got roasted chickens, smoked brisket, and seared chops slow-cooked with sauce made with apples, sausage, and onions." I continue, pointing out more, "Green beans done my way, sweet potato mash, and your favorite, Braden's mac-n-cheese casserole."

"Yum," he declares.

"If you want more, don't look here, cuz I ain't got it, kid," I tease, poking a finger into his side, causing him to playfully yelp and jump to the side.

"No prob. I think the guests are bringing stuff."

"Guests? What guests?" My voice is getting progressively louder.

Mom marches in. "What's all this noise?" she whisper-yells. Braden rolls his eyes, while I stare blankly at Mom.

Losing my own cool, I respond in kind. "Back off!" Her eyes widen before narrowing, dangerously so. I step in her direction. Unbelievably, she steps back. Yeah, something hinky is afoot. "I am *not* your catering serv—ahhh, I *am* your catering service. Well," I say, crossing my arms, "until I see that check or cash, I believe I can't be of any further service, ma'am. Gotta pay before you play, or at least eat, in this business." I raise my brow. The ball is now firmly in her court.

"Daria..." Her warning voice on steroids. Well, two can play *Don't-Fuck-With-Me*.

"Mom?"

Gauging her response, I think, *Yeah, two can play this game.* And there is some game happening. Something she doesn't want me to know about. Which means it involves me.

At the most unwelcome time, as usual, Victoria rushes in. No greeting, barely flicking me a glance. "Incoming. Guests are arriving. And wow, are the guys cuuute." Pointedly glaring at me, she says, "I get first dibs." Declaring such, with a haughty flip of her blonde hair, she rushes back out, leaving Mom in more of a frenzy than before, if that were possible.

I get an accusing glare before accusing words. "This is *all* your fault."

"Of course. It always is," I retort in a bland voice.

That has Mom blinking.

"Want to stand here fighting about it, spouting platitudes about how I am such an ungrateful, disappointing daughter, or do you want to greet your guests and leave the *servant* to get things ready?" I give her a scornful stare. "After all, this is your party. Just why did you want me to come? For this? You could have hired someone."

Palm to forehead. "But I've done this all for free. *Man*, am I stupid. I keep falling for this same setup, time and time again. When will I *ever* learn?"

I lean both hands on the counter. Dazedly, I shake my head. I stand up, straightening my spine, then face down the beauty and the beast of my heart. "Well, no more," I declare, dramatically tossing down the kitchen towel that had been draped over my shoulder.

"*Umgah*," Mom gurgles before stomping out of the room.

"OMG, Daria. Brava!" Braden proclaims, golf-clapping so Mom doesn't hear. Raised voices in greeting come from the main entryway. His sympathetic eyes swing to me. "What can I do?"

"Tell me the table is set and all the plates and tableware are out and ready?" Vacant stare. Deep sigh. "How about two migraine tablets, if they're handy."

I toss those back, ignoring Braden's pitying expression.

"Get rid of these boxes and lay out the empty platters and bowls on the island," I order, turning back to the tasks at hand.

I swear silently, *This will be the last time.* Yeah, right. Blotting away the few escaping tears, I look longingly at the door to the garage. Wishing I had the guts to escape. Closing my eyes, gathering up crumbling courage as if it is salvageable china shards, I prepare myself to endure the next several hours.

Caesar salad. I long for my Sam.

■ ■ ■

"Daria, what are you doing holed up here in the kitchen?" Mom's giggling embarrassment catches me off guard. Over an hour has passed since I've been left here by myself in the kitchen. No wine glass sits available for me to sip from, no offers of help have come my way since I've released Braden to go mingle with the guests. In fact, none have ventured here until now.

Seriously? I turn, blinking, in her direction.

"Probably sampling all the food so there's nothing left," I hear Victoria's under-breath comment.

The pursing of my lips is the only indication that I've heard. Though totally expected, it hurts. Victoria makes everything a competition. Not sure where this stems from, but it has been so for far too long to be a phase. She's my sister. I love her. Right now, I honestly can't claim to like her.

"Hey, how about this? Next time there's a family gathering, I'm bringing nothing. Not helping. Just coming, sitting, drinking, eating, and leaving. Stupid as I was for agreeing to come, even more stupid to try and make nice by dealing with the food. This has gone from being an invite to dinner with just you and Dad to a full-blown reunion and now including people I have yet to meet. I've been stuck in here, alone, as in by myself, with no one outside of Braden to help, finishing food preparations on a meal I've made that you will assume the laurels for doing while you lecture me and embarrass me every time I take a bite."

My outburst has caught both Mom and Victoria off guard.

As they stand imitating landed fish, another lady, whom I've yet to meet, steps forward. "Daria, I've heard so much about you."

I just bet you have, I long to snark, but I paste on a smile.

My heated, watery eyes and overly flushed face surely give away my feelings. I'm mad. I'm emotionally bruised once again. But now, I am done. The thing is, Mom knows it too.

The thought has me standing a bit taller.

There is something liberating about it, along with it being scary at the same time. A shuddering breath close to a sob leaves my mouth. Hastily, I press a set of knuckles to my lips. I feel the shackles unlocking me in my parental-prescribed role. A flickering look at Mom tells me she is unsure of how to deal with this, with me. What's more, Mom doesn't want to be dealing with me while the company is around.

"You must come into the other room and taste these absolutely scrumptious appetizers my son brought." The lady hooks her arm through my elbow, giving me no choice, clever woman. "I'm sure that what's more to be done here is being left in more than capable hands," she says, pointedly looking at Mom and Victoria, who now have matching looks of horror. "I'll send in Lucy to help, and Katie too." She wrinkles her nose at Mom.

"Pardon, but who are you?" I ask. "I didn't catch your name."

Her tinkling laughter tells me that this is part of the game. It's got me on extra alert. Still, the idea of leaving Mom and Victoria to finish up is too tantalizing to ignore. "I'm Bunny Bixby, a—"

"Good friend of Mom's with a son who has recently returned," I finish, groaning inside. Ignoring Victoria's predatory gleam, I flip Mom a this-isn't-over scowl before accompanying Mrs. Bixby.

BB, she tells me, as her closest friends refer to her. The person to which I just delivered a carload of desserts, though some younger guy was the one to receive them, making me late, subjecting me to Mom's wrath.

This carnie ride is beginning to make me a bit dizzy. If some crazy clown pops up, I'm going to seriously lose it.

A bit of color leaves my face, and I feel a clamping in my gut when my brain begins to put things together, realizing that those desserts weren't just meant for the Bixby bash. They were in fact meant for *this* gathering, this meal. They're here. I don't know whether to cry, scream, or laugh like a loon. Until I do, I'll just stick it out and go with the flow.

Tapping my car keys that are tucked in my pocket, I'm further empowered. I have a way out if it comes to that.

A deadly gleam reflects from my face. I flash it at Mom, tossing her a mental cackle for good measure. Her Momdar has picked up on it. With a gasp, she tosses a kitchen towel at Victoria, leaving her to finish while she hustles in our wake.

Victoria snags Mom by her blouse. "I don't know what to do," she hisses.

"Then learn. You're a smart girl, figure it out. How hard can it be? Daria is more than capable, so should you be."

Hmmm. Bunny's arm tightens her hold when she feels my trembling increase.

The tears welling in Victoria's eyes are my undoing, though I don't know why she's crying. Taking pity, I toss out, "It's all ready. Just put it on the serving dishes with the appropriate serving utensils and place it out."

Victoria nods, heaving a sigh of relief. Then she turns to the assortment of empty serving dishes and bites her nails. Deliberately, I ignore her.

As I enter the common room, a glass of wine is pressed into my hands.

BB waltzes me up to a group of strangers. "Daria, this is my husband, Robert. And these are our children." She gestures like a proud and regal queen toward four other people, most of whom are adults.

I dip my head in acknowledgment.

"Our youngest and only daughter, Lucy. She's fourteen. A late surprise but very welcomed." Lucy blushes prettily. The gleam in her eyes says she's pleased. "And these are our boys," she says, turning to three males. "From youngest to eldest, Luke, Matthew, and"—a man who has been obscured turns from his conversation with Tom, and I gasp—"Sam."

■ ■ ■

"Shhh, shh, sh. I think she's coming around. Everyone step back. Get back, I say." Sam.

I'm sprawled on the floor. He's cradling me, having pulled my head up onto his lap, pressing a cool, damp cloth to my face and neck. I blink to clear my vision, making sure all this is real and giving me time to recall events. Flambé it. I lunge into his arms, heaving an audible sigh when his strong, sturdy arms wrap around me securely.

"Sam." I breathe in the scent where my mouth and nose are firmly pressed to him.

"Shh, shh. I've got you, babe. It's gonna be okay," he croons, petting my hair.

"Nooo," I wail. "You don't understand." I sob brokenly, pulling back enough to look into his honest concern. "You've got to save me. There really is a hell." I swallow hard as I notice humor sparkling in his eyes before he banks it. "And we. Are. In it. It's here," I tell him, my eyes darting around. I must look as crazed as I feel. "It's all around us," I whisper loudly.

"Pumpkin?" I hear Dad's voice. He crouches down. "Now, take it easy. You fainted. That's all. Got overheated and excited. Bound to happen when you've got two harpies snapping at you and none to lend you a hand," he says, tossing pointed looks at someone over his shoulder.

"Let's get you up and into a chair and take it from there," Sam says, waving forward his brothers, who scurry to help me up. Once I'm on my feet, all hover until they are sure of my stability. I'm alert and stable enough to catch the looks and nonverbal exchanges between Sam and his brothers. Sam takes hold of my waist, leading me to a comfy chair, helping me ease into it. Sam scoots up an oversized ottoman and sits as near to me as possible.

"Thanks," I say all around.

Quickly, someone hands Sam a glass of water. In turn, he offers it to me, helping hold it while I take measured sips. It seems to help.

"When's the last time you've eaten?" Sam asks me. He captures my chin, forcing me to remain looking at him, only him.

When he hears Victoria snort, Sam turns a sharp, steely eye on her. It has her choking and quickly leaving the room. When he turns back to me and sees my hesitation, anger begins burning in his eyes.

"No, don't tell. Let me guess. Not since our last meal together."

My blush confirms the answer he already knows.

"You haven't eaten all day. Let me guess again. Because of this. Too busy. Some preparation ritual for coming to dine with your family."

The loud gurgling coming from my stomach gives me away.

With the snap, crackle, and popping of the cartilage in his knees, he rises like a jack-in-the-box. Within seconds, he's back, pushing a plate of food into my hands. I'm too shaky to hold it steady, so he places it on the side table and begins feeding me himself.

"I-I'll go see about getting the rest set out." Mom disappears faster than milk, eggs, and bread disappearing from the grocery store shelf when snow is predicted, dragging Katie with her.

"Aren't the appetizers simply wonderful?" Bunny gushes, nibbling on a few. "These stuffed mushrooms are to die for. I simply must have the recipe, Sam."

"Did you try the figs with bacon or the…What's the square thingies with the green slices?" Lucy asks.

"Caramelized zucchini flatbread," I supply. "There should be bacon, mushroom, and spinach pierogies."

"Like this one?" Sam asks, placing it between my lips when I open my mouth to reply. Sneaky.

"Yum. Most of everything is gone, including the blue cheese lettuce boats," Matthew says.

"Sam, you simply must give me the recipes for it all," Bunny states, looking about the room. "My son, Sam, brought the appetizers. They are his doing," she boasts.

Sam and I share a few smirky glances. Keeping his eyes locked with mine, he says clearly, "Ask Daria for them. Better yet, I'm sure they're posted on her website. She's the one who made them and the rest of what is being served. All of it." He raises an eyebrow.

I nod once, then smile.

"What nonsense!" Momdar. Mom's come back into the room, face blazing with the banked and now-releasing fury she feels is her due. "I'll admit to having the meal catered by *For the Love of Food*."

"Then I'll admit the same about the desserts," BB confesses.

Mr. Bixby wraps an arm around her waist, buzzing a sweet kiss on her cheek in pride.

Eyes travel to Sam. "As I've been trying to tell one and all but none seem to listen, I. Did. Not. Make. The appetizers…"

"*For the Love of Food?*" Matthew asks, indicating the plate he still holds.

"Precisely. The same as that wonderful blog that is all the rage," Mom says. Victoria, her bobble-head double, is at her side. "What has this to do with my daughter Daria?"

Sam flourishes his hand from me toward the audience before us, our two families.

Deep breath. "*For the Love of Food* is my side business, and from there, selective catering is another side business I do from home."

A few joyful expressions, surprise, and a few confused looks emerge following my words.

"And…" Sam encourages.

"Sam likes my pie…and me. A lot. I let him eat me…my pie… I mean." Bother. "I get naked while in his presence and make all sorts of love with him."

Proving my words, Sam lets out a war whoop, then captures my lips in one hell of a PDA, passion-filled kiss, hot enough to melt the thickest of ice sculptures.

■ ■ ■

Sam

Hello. For tonight's show, I will be playing, yet again, the undistinguished role of flycatcher. No lines necessary, just the ability to open the jaw wide enough to where the chin hits the floor.

It only took my woman fainting at my feet to get me out of my momentary stupor.

Here I was, thinking I was going to be polite and politely distant to all the females in our hosting family, as I'd tried to be with that very vexing Victoria. Victoria, as it turns out, was *not* the intended pairing of Mom's matchmaking scheme. At least I was grateful for that. I was stunned when there was a further introduction to be had. One more woman—Daria, no less.

Talk about a show stealer. If she hadn't fainted first, I may have been the one to do so.

Since I left her languorously lying in her bed this morning, her features have altered. Dramatically so. There is a stressed, harried, and angry look about her, until her flushing face loses all color before she faints at my feet. Instantly, I'm beside her, alternating between patting her cheeks and her hand, which I can't seem to release.

"Don't touch her," I yell when someone comes forward. "Bring a cool, damp cloth." Barking out orders.

"Daria?" I call her name over and over again.

From the looks being directed at me, I sense that there is a cornucopia of emotions emitting from my mouth and telegraphing on my face. Let them be confused, bewildered, befuddled. Right now, besides being pissed at those that brought this upon my love, I'm scared.

Dawning comprehension must be rising in my mom's brain, chasing away her mental fog, for I hear her sudden gasp. Fearing she, too, may be succumbing to whatever disease is plaguing my woman, just in case, I look sharply at her, finding her holding a glass of wine in one hand while the other is pressed to her lips. The color of her face has turned a zin-pink blush, working its way up to a pinot noir. Well, serves her right.

My brothers are by my side when Lucy returns with a damp cloth. I give her a quick smile of thanks.

"Ever feel you're not dealing with a full deck, like you've blown out a part of your brain in that last tissue you used?" I mutter to my brothers.

"Steady," Dad says, pressing a hand to my shoulder. He's heard too.

Interesting. In this moment of quasicrisis, my family has stepped up and stepped in, providing what it is I need without being asked. Daria's? Rubbernecking, for the most part. Only her father seems truly concerned, along with Braden, Daria's youngest brother.

"Is...Is *she* the one? The one Sam's talked about?" Mom demands, directing her questions to my siblings. No response. "Matthew?"

"Yep."

Lucy just giggles when Mom's eyes land on her.

"Luke?"

"Wow chicka chicka wow wow."

Dad chucks him in the back of the head.

"So all of this…" Mom twirls her finger, encompassing everything and everyone.

"Not. Necessary," I clip out, returning to pressing the damp cloth to Daria's face and wondering at what point do I demand an ambulance be called.

"How do you know her?" Mom's voice barely squeaks through her tightening throat.

"She's my neighbor, Mom. Had my eye on her since before purchasing the property. She was a very compelling reason to buy the place I did. Took my time getting acquainted."

"Food fairy?" Dad asks softly. I nod. He grins and snuffles his finger under and around his nose, giving Mom an I'll-tell-you-later look.

"Slow and steady wins the race," Matthew sagely remarks.

"Opportunity finally presented itself."

"Tripped into her, he means," Luke interjects.

Matthew shakes his head. "Planets fully aligned."

"You mean bodies…"

I give Luke a warning glare.

"We each seized it, took hold with both hands." Turning to Luke, I say, "Shut it. I can and ever will be able to whip your ass."

Back to Mom. "We're figuring it and ourselves out together. Won't make no difference. This is it for me."

"Oh, dear." Totally deflated. "Oh. Dear." Coming around. "Oh my dear!" She's got it. Each in their own time. Wish others would realize it before going and messing with others. Believe me, this conversation is *not* over.

"She's coming around," Lucy states. "Daria, not Mom, I mean, but Mom too." Smart kid.

Chapter 10

Sam

"Sam, you've been very helpful with Daria. Let me take her now."
Mrs. Roth leans down to take a firm hold of Daria's arm. I notice
Daria's slight flinch, as if she's wanting to pull back in resistance,
before she gives in, relenting to what she perceives as inevitable,
typical.

Deliberately, naturally, I move in such a manner as to deflect
Rachel's attempt. "Excuse me, Mrs. Roth, just where will you be
taking Daria?" Seeing her arched brows, I hasten to add, "Just
thinking I may still be of assistance." No one will be handling my
woman, even if that person is my woman's mother.

"Oh, that isn't necessary. Daria is a sturdy girl. She can manage
by herself. First, I need her in the kitchen, then I'll see her upstairs
with a plate of her own so she can have a lie-down." Mrs. Roth
shoots me a tight smile that says, *My daughter, butt out.*

Hmmm. I arch my brow with meaning. *You intend to have Daria
finish prepping, then dismiss her to her old room to eat in solitude.*

"Kitchen?" I act puzzled.

"Kitchen," Daria says with exasperation, as if the word is a
curse.

That gets a surprised face out of me. More than surprise, I'm alarmed. My woman, who loves the kitchen so much she practically made her entire main level one large kitchen, is now resisting.

"Is there a problem?" I hastily ask when Daria pushes herself up from the chair she's been resting in since she came out of her swoon.

Mrs. Roth waves me off. "No, no, no. No problem. Just need my daughter in the kitchen."

Though I know it doesn't please Mrs. Roth, I follow. Just as I thought. The reason for Daria being directed to the kitchen is to finish dinner prep. Instantly, I'm filled with rage. Daria fainted and collapsed, and her mother is still requiring and insisting Daria labor for the enjoyment of all the rest. Once finished with the chore, she will be dismissed and relegated to eating alone on an entirely different floor, separated from everyone.

Daria can't hide the tears gathering in her eyes. She knows her fate, the one set by her mother.

"Of course, Mrs. Roth, you and your other daughter, and maybe even your sons, will eagerly help. The more help, the faster this can all be assembled and set out."

Not giving the woman a chance to object, I place thumb and forefinger in my mouth and whistle loudly. Instantly, my siblings enter. "A benefit of being the eldest." I wink at Daria.

"What's up?" Matthew inquires.

"Need you to help as we finish whatever Daria directs us to do so we can all sit and enjoy this scrumptious food."

"Yeah, got it, Bro." Luke steps forward, as does Lucy. "What do you want us to do?"

"Daria?" I say, handing it over to her.

"Really, Sam, I don't ne—"

"Nonsense," I interrupt, hip-checking her onto a stool. "Now, sit here and direct," I order.

Heaving a tremulous smile, she does just that. Her first directive?

"Mom, please see that the buffet line is set up with the appropriate tableware." There could have been a standoff, but good ole Mom steps up to the plate.

"Come on, Rach, we two gals can handle that assignment," she says, tugging and smiling at the stuttering woman.

"Well, I guess you won't be needing me now." Victoria is in midtwirl on her high horse and high heels, bent on leaving the rest to the tasks, when Daria surprises even me.

"Vic, if you want to eat any of this food, you will help. No help, no food."

Victoria's face heats, making visible each of the ugly words she longs to hurl at Daria but dares not for the large audience. "Fine." She pouts, stomping over to unceremoniously dump food onto a serving plate, heedless of the mess she's making. In the midst of venting her anger, she manages to break one of the serving bowls. Even my own younger sister, along with my brothers, widens her eyes, mouthing, "OMG," at the juvenile display.

"And that, Victoria, will be taken from your allowance," Mr. Roth states, having just entered the kitchen.

The rest of us ignore Victoria's childishness. In a matter of minutes, all is completed. Each picks up a bowl or plate, proceeding into the dining room. Soon we are filing through the buffet line, filling our respective plates and finding a place to sit at the table.

"Wouldn't you be more comfortable in the quiet of your room upstairs, dear?" Rachel Roth asks Daria.

A few gasps are audible. Conversations halt at the order posed as a question. Victoria's standing in the line, plate in hand, with a look of triumph on her face. It's only when she sees my narrowed glare that she tempers her expression. Victoria's smile is totally wiped away by Daria's response.

"Not really, Mother. I rather like being around the Bixbys," she pointedly retorts.

Her reply earns inhaled breaths of horror from Team Roth and a few chuckles from Team Bixby.

"Besides, I've been my own company the past few days and find myself needing, *desiring* a bit more day company of late," she says, gifting me with a warm and genuine smile.

Leaning in, uncaring at what others say or think, I nibble on the side of her neck.

Not to be undone, Rachel Roth scans the table and produces a dramatic expression of puzzlement and concern. "There aren't enough seats at the table, Daria."

"Quite right," she agrees, plopping her gorgeous, rounded ass in one of the chairs. Immediately, I claim a seat next to hers, with Lucy on the other side. I gift my clever sister with a smile for her loyalty and support.

"Did someone miscount?" I ask, surveying the number of chairs and going through my mental check of the number of people. "Surely we can squeeze in another one."

Mrs. Roth completely ignores me. She is the proverbial hound with a bone when it comes to getting what she wants. Is this how she is with all her children, or just Daria?

"Daria, you're going to have to find another seat. Victoria needs that chair," Mrs. Roth quietly yet firmly addresses her eldest daughter.

"This isn't first-come, Sister," Victoria taunts.

"No assigned seats. No name tags," Daria quips back.

"Dibs, Daria." Victoria arches her elegantly formed brow, giving Daria that catty look she's got down pat.

Before Daria can reply by word or mouth, her father jumps in, finally. "Enough. This was meant to be a nice meal with family and friends. This silly banter is undermining all of that. None of us want to eat surrounded by it." He swings his blazing eyes at his wife, who demurely folds her hands in her lap, totally embarrassed, as she should be.

Next Mr. Roth moves to pointedly glare at Victoria. That one raises herself up as if to a challenge. The low rumbling growl that he emits does the trick. He snaps his fingers, pointing to a chair that Braden has added to the table. Rapidly, Victoria moves to it, tossing a hateful glare at Daria, who sees it but pretends she does not. Kindling for the battle that undoubtedly will ensue.

Turning to Daria, I study her while others are busy eating. With a gentling move, pushing her thick hair over her shoulder, tucking a few strands behind her ear, I cup the dangling earring. "Festive."

"That's why I selected them."

"You look wonderful in purple." Reveling in her pleased expression, I turn to find that we have a rapt audience. My siblings are tossing around pleased and knowing looks at one another, while the Roths...Strange.

"Bold looks great on you, as does sexy, if you have to wear clothing at all," I comment, loud enough for all to hear, delighting in Daria's blush and the cornucopia of expressions from those paying too close attention.

Mrs. Roth's choking I enjoy too much. Even Mom is blushing, before her lips twitch in suppressed amusement.

"Daria, how is it you came to meet Sam?" Katie inquires. The sister-in-law speaks, sending glances at Victoria and Mrs. Roth. Ah, a question she's been put up to ask.

"Sam's been my neighbor for over nine months…"

"The one who put in the outside kitchen?" Mr. Roth asks.

"Uhm-hmm." She gifts me with a smile as if I were her hero.

"Rachel, this is one heck of a meal you threw together," Dad says, tossing me a look that speaks volumes.

I lift my fork in silent salute and agreement of what he's intending. After all, it does bear repeating, as not all are convinced.

Turning to Daria, I murmur, "Got an issue being outed again?"

"Well, thank you, Robert," Mrs. Roth acknowledges. "The truth is, this is not all my doing." She flushes, sending furtive glances at her husband when he clears his throat, then pointedly glares at her.

"Oh? Bet it was Daria who did the work, then," Dad says, sitting back in his chair with a nod.

"Daria?" Mrs. Roth questions, confusion wrinkling her brow as she frowns.

"Uhm-hmm. Sam, didn't you say Daria was the one to make the appetizers?"

"Quite right, Dad. Told her that I had this family dinner tonight, and out of the goodness of her heart, she whipped up what we all sampled earlier." I place a kiss on her flushed cheek. "Feeling okay, babe?" I murmur, realizing that we both are under intense scrutiny.

"But I thought Rachel used a caterer…" Katie says, looking down at her plate, wrinkling her brow in confusion.

"*For the Love of Food?*" Mom asks with a tilt of her head. "I asked Daria to pick up and deliver. She was running late…"

"Because she was the one to drop off—ow," Luke flinches, bending down to rub his smarting shin.

"I thought I'd seen these dishes some place," Victoria chimes in. "They were on some cool foodie website…"

"*For the Love of Food,*" Daria and I say together.

"That's right," the two moms rejoin, then frown in a similar fashion.

"So what does this have to do with Daria? So she's a part-time delivery person for a five-star caterer and food blogger," Victoria says, flipping her hair in a manner suggesting she is still very much annoyed with Daria and seeking any and all opportunities to submarine her.

"Daria didn't just *deliver* the food, she *made* it. These are her culinary creations, along with the website and blog."

To me, "She *works* for them?" To Daria, "You work for them?" Wow! Victoria just doesn't seem to get it. If so, then who else sitting around the table?

Tom asks, "The person or people behind it all?"

"But I thought you were a freelance editor?" Braden asks.

"I am…"

"Then why did you refuse to help me with my term paper?" Braden demands.

"Because I edit, Braden. I don't write original works that others pawn off as their own…"

"You only create culinary masterpieces that are," I state, glancing at the two older women in the room. Completely ignoring me. Are they or anyone even listening?

"I don't need to rely on editing as much as I did before the blog took off, which brings about an occasional catering job." Daria motions to the emptying plates.

"I don't understand." Rachel Roth's words break something inside me.

Picking up my fork, I bang it against my wine glass. Instantly, I have everyone's attention; even Daria's little nephews have stopped their table-side fussing. Interesting how there was enough room for them and not Daria. Water under the bridge. For now. Dramatically,

I clear my throat, rising to stand at my place—my rightful place, beside my woman, my future wife and partner.

"I need everyone to listen and listen carefully. The food we are eating here this evening, from start to finish, regardless of who transported it, was made from scratch by Daria. It is Daria who owns and operates the blog and website *For the Love of Food*. If you are lucky to get *For the Love of Food* to whip up tasty dishes for your shindig, it is Daria who makes them."

Looking over at Daria, I ask, "Am I speaking English?" I enjoy her appreciative chuckles.

I resume my seat as Daria rises. "Since I'm coming out of the closet, or kitchen, I might as well become completely exposed. Family, guests, I have something to add. The news may shock you." Daria shrugs. "Deal with it." Deep inhaling of breath. "I am sleeping and having sex, great sex, with Sam." Turning to her jaw-dropped mother, she says levelly, "Sam's seen me naked, many times. He likes me naked."

"I like it, like her. Daria. Naked. Love the sex we have too. Plan to have more tonight as soon as we get home," I add wickedly.

■ ■ ■

Daria

"Did you see their faces?" I gasp through my laughter and tears. "I still think some aren't convinced. They'll wake up tomorrow believing this day has been a mirage, a fig in their imagination."

"Don't you mean figment?"

"Nope, a fig. An unusual fruit so confusing and curious just the same, many are reluctant to sample let alone try again or believe." Chuckling.

"Yeah, it was pretty funny. Not sure how to describe their

emotions. More like frozen video moments." Sam starts making weird faces and holding the look just a bit too long.

I peal with laughter. "Grape jelly, my sides hurt from all the laughing."

"Good. It looks good on you."

I quirk a brow.

"Laughter. And now I'm thinking grape jelly too. We'll have to experiment. You know, variants and all..." His face clouds over. "You sure you're okay? No lingering effects..."

"From my swoon?" I ask, then shake my head. "There could be some real fallout, though, from the rest that's come to light," I warn.

Sam sobers and nods before giving me a look of approval. Another of respect. Leaning over, he whispers huskily, "Damn, babe." Placing a hand on the back of my head, he pulls my face closer still for one of his slow, roasting kisses that tend to quick-fire my brain and send a rush of pooling moisture down below. "I was really proud of you. Still am." His lips tease mine when he pulls slightly back.

I smile.

■ ■ ■

Sam

Yeah, I am proud of my woman. I know she has hang-ups regarding her weight. Figured it mostly stemmed from her upbringing and what society thinks is and isn't vogue. Understanding was never more pointedly made clear than in watching her family dynamic.

Daria was right. She is invisible.

Whether it is from their desire to protect her or to remove her to lessen their own embarrassment over her size or their believed failing, that is still a bit unclear. Even her sister-in-law has adopted the family habit of ignoring Daria or finding a place for her to fit in by relegating her to the kitchen, where she remains hidden and unseen. Not a full write-off, but a brush-off, and being placed out of sight is a write-off all the same.

Whatever. It was well over an hour after my family's arrival that we actually were introduced to Daria. And that took work on Mom's part, fetching Daria, who had been consigned to the kitchen, working her ass off while all else drank, conversed, and nibbled on the appetizers *she* had made while expressing their delight to me, the one who carried them in.

"Do you think our moms will remain friends?" Daria asks.

I shrug. "Something they will have to figure out on their own, without their children's interference. Well, one thing's for sure, they're going to have to review their dynamic. In fact, I think my dad, and hopefully yours too, will be having a sit-down with their lady loves. We both know that they operate out of a sense of love and desire to see their children successful and happy. That motherly zeal can place them in blinders they are unaware they have on until the proverbial crash."

"Meddling can have severe consequences." Daria leans her head against the car window as I drive us home. "All in all, I'm glad we stayed, stayed through to the end."

"Yeah?"

"Uhm-hmm. Really. I was about ready to march out to my car and leave when your mom came in the kitchen. Mom had come in with Victoria, admonishing me for hiding in the kitchen instead of being with the others." A watery swallow. A hasty blinking of eyes. "Thing is, it was a lie. I was right where she intended me to be." A sob-laugh breaks from her lips. Quickly, she presses her knuckles to them.

"Daria?" Now I'm concerned again. Have to remind myself that deep wounds that have had a lifetime of being created will need time to heal. Won't be happening overnight. The scab has been ripped off, allowing some of the putrid pus to drain. One thing's for sure, Daria and her mom, and at some point Daria and Victoria, will have to sit down and have a heart-to-heart.

As I drive one-handed, using my other to touch Daria, I recall the rest of that rather interesting dining experience.

Chapter 11

Daria

The abrasiveness of his whiskers against my inner thighs as he feasts, slurping, licking, and tugging on my rather plump, raspberry pearl of a clit, is enough to get me off. Totally cosmic on a whole new level when still nestled in my folds, his voice vibrates through that sensitized flesh.

"Yum, this is the dessert I was after. Babe, the flavor of Daria always wins out, even next to your divine food." Tongue licks its way back to front, spearing the jelly-filled hole before lingering on that swollen berry. "Daria, you are a complete feast."

Morning sex is always great with Sam. This morning's morning-after sex, even more so.

Though Sam arrived at my parents' with his family, we left together in my car. Sam insisted on driving. He even backed up into the garage to make emptying the car of what remained of the meal—empty dirty dishes—easier. What had not been consumed had been claimed, repackaged for guests to take home or to remain in Mom's fridge to be consumed later. We brought no leftovers home.

Mom's dirty tableware had been stacked in the dishwasher, my used and unrinsed plates and platters unceremoniously placed in the boxes used to carry them in before being run out to my car. Gee, thanks.

"Leave it," Sam said, drawing me into the house by my hand. "It'll keep. I'll help with it later."

Making for the bedroom, Sam proceeded to undress me as if I were a sleepy child in need of assistance. Once we both were naked, he eased us under the covers, pulling me into his arms. Only then did I let out a sigh.

"You're exhausted, babe. Ease your body and your mind tonight. We'll work on the heart and soul later, after we wake."

I placed a kiss over his very generous heart. Cupped Frank with my hand.

"I am sooo glad that is over." Another sigh. "Even more glad that you're here with me."

A quick smack of a kiss on my head, and I'm falling into a blissful slumber, vaguely hearing, "We'll debrief and strategize about any potential fallout."

Great. Battle plans.

■ ■ ■

Five days later. Gazing out of my office window, I find myself oddly uninterested in my blog. Even too distracted to work on my current novel. That in itself is telling. Instead, my mind drifts back to the point when my gallant knight, Sam, spilled the proverbial beans, or in the case of our collective families, put all the shuffled pieces together.

I'm still not convinced that they all got it. Must the third time be the charm?

"Maybe it isn't that they don't get it. It's probably more along the lines that they don't want to get it. Means they'll have to do plenty of self-reflecting. What they *should* find won't be pretty.

People get angry when confronted with the reality of the lie they've been using to fool themselves," Sam said.

"Then what?"

He shrugged. "Depends, babe. Either they'll come around, or they won't. You don't have to deal with toxic people. You can love people and not like them. As an adult, you set the terms on how you will interact with others and they with you. There is nothing in the rulebook that says you have to be a doormat."

Replaying the event over and over in my mind makes for restless nights and chaotic days.

"You need some sort of resolution, babe," Sam said when I told him of my troubles. "Seems to me you got two options. Let them come to you, or you go and confront them."

"Other options?" I chewed on my lower lip like it was too-tough taffy. Sam's eyes narrowed on the spot, then he reached over, using his thumb to extract my lip.

"Change zip codes?" Hah! Hmm. Thinking, thinking…tapping my chin while still thinking.

"How about Mars. Wanna go?" I happily suggested. Less than half kidding. "Weightlessness—"

The cracking of his hand on my naked ass abruptly ended the thought and my words.

"None of that. You will not continue to disrespect what I love by downing yourself with statements seemingly pithy and humorous. Don't. Write. Yourself. Off."

■ ■ ■

My mind is still consumed with what went down that evening. Nearly a week later, it keeps going back. I must be processing it. That's the only way I can explain it.

"Get the picture? All of it?" Sam said to one and all, half

tauntingly, half irritated that it had come down to this. Those words keep repeating over and over in my head. More so, what followed the reveal.

"Well, now that is all cleared up…" Mom sighed with nonchalant lack of interest, pushing up from the table, pointedly looking at me. "Daria will clear the table, and then we shall have dessert and coffee in the parlor, once that has been set up."

Sam was thunderstruck, but any words he was about to spout were cut off by Dad.

"Sit right where you are, Daria," Dad instructed.

I stayed sitting as told, as any dutiful daughter would, even if the daughter is on the downside of her twenties.

Turning to Mom, he said, "Wife, I think our family who've been sitting on their laurels and stealing another's, including you, for far too long this evening can assist with that. Daria deserves the rest, after all she's done for us. Don't you think?" Meaningful, no-nonsense laser eyes were directed at all the adult Roth family members.

Not waiting for a reply, he turned to the rest. "While my family clears and sets up, why don't the rest of us go sit in the parlor. We've got a nice fire going and brandy and other winter and standard libations for those interested in an after-dinner nip."

Sam is my number-one hero. Dad—coming in a clear second place just then. He even managed to buzz my cheek and pat it before moving off, assuming those invited would follow. The Bixby clan picked up their service, trotting into the kitchen before joining us in the parlor.

"I *hate* you right now!" Victoria hissed as she passed me by, her face morphing into some scary she-monster, what with her curled upper lip and snarling mouth. The glowering eyes matched perfectly.

"Is that what's fueling your behavior? Behavior not really any different from any other time? So how am I to know, Victoria, if it's love or hate you truly feel?"

That had Victoria's forward motion coming to a dead halt, her eyes rapidly blinking in confusion.

"So let's end this tettery-tottery horror-go-round of a ride," I continued. "I want off. No more, Victoria! You're my sister. Always will be. I've loved you since before you were a bump in Mom's belly. Will always love you. Since you're so into being candid, let me return in kind. I love you. Right now? Don't like you much. Whatever this is," I said with wild, waving, gesticulating hands, "I'm done with it. The snarky, selfish, self-serving attitude."

Suddenly, I was both empowered and exhausted in a way I'd never really experienced before. It fueled me on, recklessly so.

"Don't bring me down ever again with your words, deeds, and actions. Not only is it hurtful, it's spiteful, vindictive, and so beneath the person you should be. If you can't be nice and civil, then leave me the hazelnut alone." Now it was my turn to turn and walk away, to turn and leave her stewing in her muddle puddle.

After I extracted the fork from my mouth that was filled with spice cake and whipped-cream icing, Mom ruined the bliss with a hiss. I know it's bad when she merely looks at my chipmunk cheeks midchew and then to what's left on my plate.

"Daria, you've hurt your sister," Mom charged.

She must have stumbled over the stuttering remains of Victoria.

"Mom, butt out. Victoria got what she deserved. She knows it. She's processing and, hope against all hope, will gain insight, making her a better person." I heaved a sigh through cream-coated lips, my tongue desperately seeking the lingering buttery residue before bite two.

"What's got into you?" Mom was not wanting to leave it alone. Claws were out for one of her damaged cubs. What about me?

"Let's just say…I'm done with being on the receiving end of things." Sam fed me another bite. I opened my mouth like a baby bird. "With the exception of that, and a few other things," I mumbled around the bite, hand held over my mouth, winging looks at Sam. His facial response made me blush.

"She's crushed, Daria. Utterly devastated."

"The truth can be hard to swallow at times, Mom," I said, dramatically swallowing that bit of cake. Taking a sip of coffee. Dabbing the festive napkin on my mouth. Peering up at the woman who gave birth to me.

"Mom. What's crushing is that you are more concerned about me calling her out for the bitch she's been this evening instead of understanding that she and *you* have said things and have acted worse toward me for decades, this evening being no exception. At least I did it in relative privacy." I arched an eyebrow. "Yet here you are, speaking such things to me in front of Sam and his family. Where's your apology? Where's hers?"

It was as if I'd bitch-slapped her.

In a daze, she staggered away.

Puckering the space between my brows until Sam soothed it smooth with a firm but gentle thumb, I wondered if she might indeed be a bit tipsy.

I didn't speak to her for the rest of the evening. She didn't even see me before leaving to say thanks or goodbye. Believe me, I'll be billing her for my services. Maybe that will make my point, since nothing else seems to penetrate that thick wall of indifference.

■ ■ ■

I'm so into my retrospective, I don't notice the car pulling into the drive until it is simply there.

Mom.

Releasing an audible groan, I slam my hands on my desk before pushing myself up to answer the door. Her coming to the front door speaks volumes.

Only guests came to the front.

She's not here for a social call. Not here as family. She's here on business. Well, that makes two. Snatching up the invoice for that evening's meal and the portion I feel she is responsible for, I march out of my office.

I hide in the hall, waiting for the doorbell to chime. It does. Instead of directly going to the door, I decide brushing my teeth and checking my braided hair are preferable. Vindictive me makes her ring twice. Still reeling from that night, I'm in no mood to rush and kiss her feet, or her ass.

Calmly, I open the door, blocking her entry.

"Daria."

"Mom. What a surprise." Soto voce.

We both stand here, silent and waiting. We can wait for Godot for all I care.

"It took you long enough to answer the door. You going to make me—"

I slam the door.

Relishing the look of wide-eyed, oh-lipped surprise on her face, I just stand here. Waiting.

I only open the door again when she knocks—three times. "Mom. What a surprise."

"Daria."

"What brings you here? Just in the neighborhood?" My cheery voice confuses her, as it is meant to.

"You haven't been accepting my calls."

"Uhm-hmm."

"Aren't you going to allow me in?"

She peers around me to see what she can of the interior. In the fashion of many Asian homes, there is a wall running horizontally opposite the door just inside, preventing those at the door from looking inside the dwelling proper. Not only is it a way to maintain privacy, but it's also a trap for demons and spirits bent on ill doings. Evil spirits are unable to make the jag around the corner. Must be working, because it has and is keeping her out.

"That all depends." Stoicism at its best.

Her slight head shake, along with blinking eyes, is her Mom-speak for, "What?"

Sighing audibly while beaming a wide, closed-lipped smile, I say, "Mom. I've lived here for three years. In those three years, you've never once stepped inside or been over that I've been aware. Even when invited, which you have been numerous times, you've kept your distance." I hold my hand up, staving off her words when she's about to speak. "You've got your excuses, but three years is a bit long to draw them out. Now you've come. Alone. So I've got to ask before I permit you beyond the threshold. Why?"

Her fists are tightly held at her sides. "Since you won't return my calls, I've decided to come to discuss your deplorable behavior—"

Slamming the door feels good. Throwing the deadbolt with an audible *chick*, even better.

I'll mail her the da…dolmas invoice. I skip down to the office to do just that. I'll need to find an envelope and stamp.

Rapid pounding on the door is combined with her rising vocalizing volume. "Daria! Open this door at once. I demand you open this door. I. Am. Your. Mother. Let me in…"

Not by the hairs on my chinny chin chin.

"I'm not leaving until you open this door. Daria! Do you hear me?"

Yep. And all the neighbors too.

Everyone is watching her continuing tantrum until she drives away.

Not now, possibly ever, will I allow such venom into my home, my sanctuary. This is not the snake bringing knowledge, something I rather respect. This is the poison apple of another story bent on she-devil knows what. That's the mystery I have yet to solve.

Later, much later, on light feet, I skip my way to the mailbox, depositing the outgoing bill. Lobster bisque, I'll take her mom ass to small claims if she doesn't pay.

■ ■ ■

"Ten minutes. That's how long she stood there, steaming and spewing on my doorstep, raising her voice and pounding on my door, ringing the doorbell. At one point, I actually considered calling the cops. I remained undeterred," I say, filling in Sam when he came to dinner tonight.

"I would have loved to have seen the look on her face. Guess that explains it." A strange look comes over his face.

"What?"

"Uhm, Daria? When was the last time you checked your food blog?"

It's the tone more than the words that has me on alert. Rapidly, I gain my feet, running to my office. Sam, as ever, is on my tail.

"Holy..." Sam has not been in my office. "This...This is where you work? Of course it is. Often I see you silhouetted in the double expanse of windows, seated at this desk, facing the computer. Never did I think the space would be so...like this," he breathes.

"Another modification to the standard floor plan."

"Wow."

Being as it's a two-storied home and I didn't see myself ever finding a person to put a ring on it or having kids, I created instead a two-story library-office of my dreams. Instead of Tuscan, I went with an English style. Dark wood and leather. The ceiling had been opened, using the upstairs bedroom to create a two-storied room with columns supporting an upper balcony that rings the space, ending at a spiral staircase.

Floor-to-ceiling book and display cases dominate the walls, complete with ladders on rollers. Again, this room has a fireplace, with Persian rugs laying in front ringed with deep, dark, ox-blood leather seating. Display tables are strategically placed housing keepsakes. There is a small conference table for when I need to spread out materials or confer with clients. Paintings hang from selected niches and places, breaking up the large number of books, keeping the place from looking chaotic and instead giving it the look of a room well used, the kind found within a grand English country estate.

The fact that Sam does not linger, exploring the space, tells me that this is serious.

Hip-to-hip we sit, cursing the computer, wishing the speedy thing were speedier yet. Nerves have my fingers fumbling, until Sam places a steadying hand on my back. Access achieved, I sit in shock, reading the recent novel of a comment.

"How could she do this to me?" I wail, dipping my forehead to rest against the edge of my desk. Sam alternates between caressing my back and petting my head and hair.

"I take it, in the past, chastisement was readily meted out in public," Sam states, his fury barely contained.

Nodding, I affirm, "Either she is clueless or actually prefers it. She thinks embarrassing me by drawing attention to this"—sweeping a hand from my head to my toes—"draws attention away from her.

Haven't fully figured that one out. Her best moments, most humiliating chastisements, have always been conducted in public. You saw how she was in the privacy of her home with friends."

"Typically that bad?"

I snort. "That was tame."

"Another reason you hide?"

Again, I nod. "The fear of her striking out, and doing so in public…" I close my eyes to block out the humiliation many of those moments brought down upon my head. "It wasn't just that she was ashamed of me, but she had to let all who could hear know it as well."

I tell him of the time I ran out to grab an item at the store, an ingredient I hadn't had enough of and was in desperate need of. It was part of the food being made for my mom's birthday party.

Without thought as to what I was wearing, sloppy sweats and a sweatshirt, I snatched up my keys, intent on dashing in and out of the store. While there, I ran into Mom. Not only would she not stop scolding me on my attire and how much more gargantuan and unappealing it made me—so much so that I'd never get a man and remain unloved all my life—she insisted that I stand in a different checkout line. One that was farthest away from her. All the while drawing more attention to her shamefully fat, ugly daughter.

"Daria, this is a potentially larger audience than just those inside the store…"

"Sam, it might have begun there, but people talk. I was the talk for weeks after. Everywhere I went people brought it up. Whispered to others behind their hands. Some openly smirked while eyeing me up and down. Thinking they had a right to add to Mom's criticisms. But you're right. The entire world can see this." I gesture helplessly at the screen.

RachRoth: Daria, since you won't answer your phone and slammed the door in my face, twice, it is my hope that this reaches you. I am your mother. You have shamefully disrespected me. Keeping secrets. Refusing a mother's loving advice and concern for her eldest daughter. Attempting to steal your sister's beau. Belittling her while in the company of friends. Hurting her feelings cruelly. Didn't even spend time with your other siblings and dear nephews. Your tardiness nearly ruining the entire evening with the lack of food. Food not ready to serve, but still in need of final preparation. Was it so much to ask that you bring the food for our little soiree? Was it too much to help clear the table and prep for dessert? Was it too much to ask that you retreat from guests and your young nephews while so obviously ill and claiming exhaustion? You complain about having to help with the meal. What else have you to do with your time? You aren't married. Never will likely be, what with your unseemly weight. You spend most of your life inside your home. Must it take the promise of food, a meal, to bring you out of your hole? Why will you not even let me into your house? I am your mother. You owe me an apology. I am waiting.

My harsh laugh turns into crazed cackles that morph further into full-out sobs. Burying my face in my hands, I don't realize that I'm in Sam's arms until I begin to calm and am able to feel beyond the pain that has seized my heart. How did I get into his lap?

"Write her off, babe. Write. Her. Off. Don't let her affect you, making you think that what she thinks is true or real." Sam is frantic with rage, suppressing it for my sake.

"I can't, Sam. I can no more write her off than I can respond to her posting." My voice is ragged, filled with agonizing pain. "She's my mother. She's a human being. I can't disrespect her that way."

"To get beyond this, you will have to confront her. That isn't disrespect."

He cups my cheeks with his large, manly hands. As he lowers his lips in that descent of anticipation, something on the computer screen catches his attention. He starts grinning before his lips can tease mine.

"Going higher, or at least not descending, in the face of a misdirected foe who's also family makes me admire you all the more. Seems a few do not have your scruples," he says.

His eyes dart to the screen once more.

Sam kisses me into tomorrow before I discover what he's noticed.

"Cyber knights. I have blog banshees, champions willing to take on the spewing dragon that has taken over my mother," I say in awe.

I start weeping more. There before my swollen, watery, red eyes is the written, well-typed evidence.

Comment: For shame, to dress down someone in such a fashion. This is NOT the forum for such action. Take it elsewhere.

Comment: Berate yourself, RachRoth, not your daughter.

Comment: Poor pity you, RR. Get the facts right, righteous b**ch.

Comment: Who invites family to dinner and then demands another bring the food to feed all? Seriously? And you're mad? If it were me, I'd be using poison as one of the ingredients. Beware the cookies…

Comment: What's your real beef? Seek therapy—for yourself.

Comment: RachRoth, does your head spin around backward too?

On and on they continue. Finally, I can read no more.

Chapter 12

Sam

Deliberately and unannounced, once again I find myself standing on the Roths' front door stoop, waiting for admittance into the dragon's lair. Staccato steps accompanied by a heavier shoe rapidly approach.

"Oh, hmm, look who's here," Mrs. Roth states. Clearly, she isn't happy to see me. "Are you here to see Victoria?"

I shake my head.

Yeah, I see that one's head popping back out of sight. Fury is her mask.

"Pardon my sudden appearance, Mrs. Roth, Mr. Roth. I hope my coming here this way and at this hour isn't an inconvenience, but I do wish to speak to both of you." I may be knocking on thirty, but I know well the manners my mother drilled into me. She'd have my scalp if I disregarded them, particularly here and now.

"Uh…" Mrs. Roth utters, chewing her lower lip like her daughter as she casts an uncertain look at her husband. She's seen my resolute expression. It makes her nervous and wary. She should be.

David Roth pushes in front of his wife, extending his hand. "Sam, there is no problem, and we will make time." Shaking my hand, he says, "Come in. Come in, please." He steps back, opening the door wider to allow entrance.

I follow them into the parlor, and they offer me a seat near the fire. Gratefully, I accept a tumbler of whiskey.

"The reason for my coming is simple. Daria—"

"Sent you to apologize. I knew it," huffs Mrs. Roth. "Well, you can go straight back—"

"Mrs. Roth…Mrs. Roth, you have it all wrong. Daria doesn't even know I'm here, that I had any intention of coming here this way."

She blows out an exasperated breath.

"Enough, Rachel! Sit down and allow this young man to fully speak without interruption. Obviously what he plans on saying is important enough to have him coming over."

I shoot the man a grateful look, one he acknowledges before his features harden when directing them at his wife.

Twin red dots emerge on the apples of Mrs. Roth's cheeks. Her husband's words have the effect of shutting her up. Though she throws eye daggers at him, she demurely folds her hands in her lap before turning her attention to me. She's a tiger, deceptively at ease yet ready to pounce without warning.

"As I was saying…Daria doesn't know I'm here, but I will be telling her. As an outsider, what is going on between her and you is none of my business. I get that. Get this. As one who loves her… I'm making it my business."

I wonder if anyone my age has ever addressed Mrs. Roth so. Get used to it, lady. There's more to come.

"Daria loves you and all in her family. I hope that love is re-ciprocated." Seeing her look of outrage, I continue, "Yes, from my brief encounter with you and her and some of the Roth family, your and their love for Daria is questionable. Regardless, Mrs. Roth, you and some of her family have become the source of her greatest pain. She suffers. I'm here to ask that you find a way to repair the damage that is threatening to undermine what is left of your relationship."

Deep breaths. There. I've said it. Now let the avalanche begin. Either it will work to help clear things up or leave me dead.

Seconds turn to minutes, and those…Mr. Roth, with his continued silence and piercing gaze focusing on his wife, is insisting that she be the one to engage. I'm more interested in the emotions that telegraph across the woman's face.

"Why?"

The one word spoken by the woman leaves me confused.

"Why?" I echo the word. Sliding to the edge of my seat, I say, "Daria has suffered enough, too much. It's obvious to those who witness your public rebuking of your daughter that you do not approve of her, do not accept her as she is and for what she is. Some question your love, let alone if you even like the daughter you birthed."

Mrs. Roth waves her hand, dismissing my words.

I tilt my head. Now I'm confused.

"No, not that. We'll return to that…Why, Sam Bixby, why do you love her? Love Daria. How could you or anyone love…love *that*?"

Darting a look over at Mr. Roth, I see the man's expression mirrors my own. Did we hear her correctly?

Blinking back my growing rage, I just have to know. "Mrs. Roth, are you questioning my sincerity toward Daria, or are you questioning that anyone could possibly ever love her?" Both are insulting. One is outrageous. "Daria is a remarkable person. She's one of a kind. When the gods created her, they threw away the mold. For you see, there was no way to improve upon such perfection—" My poetic eloquence, being what it is, is rudely interrupted by inelegant female snorting. "Excuse me, Mrs. Roth? Do you even know your own daughter? If you truly did, you would heartily agree."

"Why, the nerve...Of course I know my daughter! I gave birth to her, saw her raised and cared for. I am more than aware of who and what she is...her flaws..."

"Pardon me for saying that I have doubts on that score. If your idea was to raise a child without flaws, then you've failed...miserably, I might add." Holding up a hand at her outraged gasp, I continue, "Hear me out. All of us are flawed. None of us are perfect. The beauty of love is that we love the entire person, flaws and all. Her one great flaw is that Daria is damaged inside. Her soul and her heart. I seek to lessen that pain and to help her heal..."

"How can you possibly love her? Daria is *fat*..."

"What are you saying? Daria can't be loved because of her weight? That's utter nonsense! It's like saying *you* can't be loved because of your barbed tongue, or Victoria because of her self-centeredness and willingness to belittle Daria in public. I find those character flaws more unappealing and off-putting than Daria's physical size, which I happen to love and enjoy."

Yeah, I hear the smothered gasp coming from outside the room. Victoria, the little sneak, has been spying.

"I know Daria's physically large. So what? I happen to adore her size. As long as she's healthy, her size doesn't and will not matter. Would you claim a person with different-colored hair or eyes or different-sized feet was unlovable? Unworthy of love? How about a person missing a limb or in a wheelchair or with a physical deformity? Would you write them off the way you've written off your own daughter?"

My words seem to please Mr. Roth.

Mrs. Roth is a different case.

I don't let up. "Since you know so much about what you consider Daria's flaws, surely you must be aware of how incredible she is. Daria is a woman of great passion and depth of feeling. It's in all she does. One look at her garden, the interior of her home, one taste of her food is all it takes to realize that. The fact is, the closer you look at what she has created, the more you come away with a new perspective on how creative and talented and genuinely good she is. Makes me desire a lifetime of learning the full depths of her. Even then I wonder if it will be enough time."

"Then why are you here, if you love her, as you say?"

Hasn't the woman been listening?

"I want her to be fully happy. She's had a lifetime of being rejected by most of those who should have accepted her. Daria is even reluctant to value and accept herself. I mean to see that change. I have been seeing progress, great progress, on that score." Taking a deep breath, I add, "Mrs. Roth, Daria can be happier still if *all* the people she loves would only accept her. Accept her as she is and not judge her by some mold they've created for her that will never fit, would have never fit her, regardless—"

"You talk about mending fences, Mr. Bixby. What you don't speak to is how Daria has hurt *me*, publicly so. At every turn, all of her life, she's been an embarrassment."

Hmm.

My eyes scan the walls and tabletops in the room. Finally, landing on what I seek, I rise from my chair. "Do you mind?" I ask, indicating a photo collage. "Mom has papered the hallway walls of her home with such pictures. Family. Photos of us kids all through the years. Some in groups and at special times in our lives. Others individually. There were the three of us boys for the longest time until Lucy was conceived and born. Our surprise baby. One that could have made Mom bitter and fretful for having a child when she wasn't meant to. Instead, she, and we in turn, saw it and Lucy as a blessing. Life wouldn't be the same without her."

Pictures say thousands of words. Every photo that includes Daria has her positioned behind the others or shielded in some way, blocking all or most of her save her face. I see no individual photos of just her. No birthday pictures. No holiday photos or special occasion photos such as graduation, prom.

"It was always a struggle getting Daria in front of the camera. That's why…She was always a chubby child. Her first Halloween, I dressed her as a pumpkin. The nickname stuck. *Humph*. Not much has changed on that score, only her size. Instead of being a little pumpkin, she is a huge, round one. Doesn't matter what I say or what I do…"

My shaking head has her stopping. "It had and has everything to do with who and what she is, Mrs. Roth. Daria has told me some about her aunt Alphia."

Mrs. Roth's pinched lips and cool eyes say lots. "Two peas in a pod. Once together, it was hard pulling them apart," she mutters. Jealousy?

"Yeah, Daria speaks of their similarities. How it was her aunt that cultivated her love for gardening and kitchen witchery while fueling her imagination and knowledge through books and travel."

"Daria's kitchen skills quickly surpassed Rachel's, until it was Daria doing nearly all the cooking. Seem to recall that she was the one to mow the lawn and tend the garden and yard during the growing months," Mr. Roth adds as he rubbed his chin, considering. "Boys would complain and pitch a fit when directed to that chore. Daria readily went at it. Gave her that portion of the boys' allowance for her effort—"

"Both fat," Mrs. Roth interrupts her husband.

Seeing something else hanging from the wall, I step closer to inspect. An old photograph taken at the turn of the century, and others dating from the fifties and seventies, if the fashions worn are a clue. "Are these people family?" I ask.

"Really, Mr. Bixby, is this how you planned on spending our time and yours, perusing old family pictures?" Her words gain her a glare from Mr. Roth.

"If they will help make my point and put a bit of sense into you, then yes. Look, Mrs. Roth. You might not realize it, but you are in danger. Danger of losing one of your children irrevocably. There is considerable damage to your relationship with the woman that I love. It's fixable…Now. Later?" I shrug my shoulders.

"The thing to ask yourself, wife, is what is it worth to you to not be at odds with our Daria? What is Daria's worth? Are you willing to be permanently estranged from her for the rest of our lives? That's what Sam is saying. This is the point, the precipice you are at."

"She humiliated me. Online. The whole world knows of it… and everyone in this community. They're laughing at me. Me. I see them whispering behind their hands and talking softly but loud enough for me to hear. Others say such rude things to me, as if they have a right to judge."

"So you've had a taste. A taste of what Daria has had to endure her entire life, encouraged by her own mother." At least the father gets it. "You, wife, were the one to put your foot in it. Your private…whatever this is…could have remained private, save for embarrassing us all when we had the Bixbys over, if not for you."

"What was I to do? She refused my calls, slammed the door in my face, twice, when I went to her…" she rants while rapidly blinking back pity tears.

"This was about getting her attention? More about getting your way regardless of the consequences. Being right. Wife, you are reaping what you've sown. Too bad if it isn't what you wanted or expected," Mr. Roth counters. Turning to me, he says, "In answer to your questions, those are pictures of my wife's family. And I know what you're trying to say…"

"What? What are you two alluding to? What's your point?"

Obtuse much? I want to ask.

"Large, full-figured, Rubenesque women run in your family. Daria's shape and size come naturally. I will agree, some of it can be attributed to a bit of overindulgence or depression, but not all of it. Would you agree?" I ask pointedly, drilling my eyes on the fuming woman.

"Agree? What does that have to do with things? Besides, it doesn't have to be that way for Daria. With a bit of self-control and firm resolve and discipline and fewer bites of food—"

"All this you have made a part of your parenting litany since she was a baby. You sought to chastise her, humiliate her, body-shame her for something she has no hand in controlling—her genetics. You might as well have criticized her for breathing. Can't stop that either. Breathing, like eating, must be done, or we die. Or would you prefer that be Daria's lot?"

That has her paling.

Twisting my wrist to view my watch, I finish with, "I know I've taken up plenty of your time. Given you plenty to chew on. You may be mad. Be mad at yourself. Can't be angry at Daria for the public mess you find yourself in just now. You were the one to make it and step in the proverbial pile of dog shit. It stinks. Instead of being mad about it, clean it up. You shouldn't expect Daria to."

Chapter 13

Sam

"You did what?" Daria demands.

"I don't need to repeat myself, Daria. You heard what I said." Talk about coitus interruptus. "Okay, I concede the timing's a bit strange…"

Her giggles catch me off guard. At least she doesn't appear to be mad. I pull back my head, where I placed it tucked deep into her neck and hair.

"Mind telling me what you were thinking?"

Yeah, I see the smirk on her kiss-swollen lips.

My eyes dip lower, to the love bite on the side of her neck and the other that sits above her heart. Yeah, I love leaving myself on her canvas. I so enjoy her and my work. Spotting the next placement, I begin nibbling and licking my way to that area.

"I was thinking that I like that there is nothing between us. With that being the case physically," I continue, rubbing my naked body over her luscious one as she continues to lay beneath me, making my point, "I thought to keep it so in all ways. This relationship is gonna be founded on honesty and clear and transparent communication. I guess my subconscious blurted it out. Consider it another type of premature ejaculation."

Her smirk intensifies. She turns her face away hastily to hide the laugh that threatens to spill out. It jiggles her body, making the vibration ripple through our touching and joining flesh.

"Oh, I get it. Don't think I can multitask, operate with two heads at one time? Well, thank you very much, I'll have you know that this head here," I say, tapping my noggin, "can function just fine when Mr. Frank B. Swellington is otherwise actively engaged."

"Prove it," my lady love commands, shaking out her hair in a sultry, sexy sort of way.

And I do.

■ ■ ■

"So is there a plan?" Daria cautiously ventures later over breakfast.

Yeah, I get her reasons for it. I'd be cautious too. How many times do you suffer getting burned before realizing that placing your hand in the fire comes with consequences? Why continue the torture? Why endure it?

"Gotta meet, babe. No getting around that. Face-to-face is how it should be. The question is where. Can't be in public, not for what could come out or go down." Her shoulders lift and lower in heavy relief. "Your parents' place?" I shake my head. "Nah, too many memories. Besides, it's her territory. Puts you at a disadvantage. Then there is here." I hold up my hand in order to finish my thought. "Your territory. Gotta be fair. Besides, I don't want her first inside visit bringing bad mojo into this castle of joy."

"So…where?" she presses.

"My place. Neutral ground. Private. Easily accessible to both parties."

Daria is back to chewing on her lower lip. Leaning in, I use my teeth to extract and my tongue to soothe.

"Babe?"

She's thinking, then nodding. Giving me a tentative smile that begins to grow. "Yeah. I'm game if she is. Is it to be only her, or will the others be coming too?"

"Your dad. Got to allow all parties to be equally balanced. You've got..."

"You, and Mom will have Dad. I'm good with it. So now the place has been decided...The question is when."

■ ■ ■

Daria

The location for our future meet is quickly agreed upon. Sam, again, does the honors of making that contact, going through Dad. The when of it...Not until after the New Year. Whether it is another jab at me or simply convenient, Mom and Dad have decided to fly to London for Christmas and ring in the New Year there. Tom and his brood, along with Victoria and Braden, are invited to join them. I am not.

"You've traveled extensively as it is, Daria. Besides, the way things are between us just now..." Mom sounds off in the message left on my answering machine. Yeah, I still insist on having a landline. "Not sure if you'd be comfortable on that long of a flight, and we will *not* pay for two seats when one should really do, but there again—"

Sam's arm comes around me. His finger presses the off button before he pulls me away from the answering machine.

"I can fit in a regular seat. Don't need an extension belt unless the plane is owned by the airline that flies nonstop to that sunny state of Florida. Besides, I've been to London. Aunt Alphia and I went several times."

To his credit, Sam allows me to process. Another knife plunged deep within my heart.

"This isn't sour grapes, Sam. All in all, given a choice, I would rather be spending the holidays with you..."

"If? Daria, those puppy-dog eyes say there is an *if* statement left unspoken."

"If you don't have any other plans..."

Sam appears to be caught between anger, pity, and rapture, leaving me confused. Scared. Wondering which one will win out.

"Since I'm single and all grown up, I tend to spend Christmas Eve or Christmas Day over at Mom and Dad's. New Years, there's usually a party with my friends. Now that I've got my own company, that includes partners, employees, and clients..."

"You thinking you want to have a bash for them? How many? Where? When?"

Chuckling, Sam answers all my questions, tilting his head. "What are you thinking, babe?"

"New traditions need to be started well if you plan on continuing them. Don't you think?" I ask. Sam gives me a considering look. "Want to host it here? Then another for your family and one for your friends?" I shock both myself and him with my offer.

Ecstatic joy lights up Sam's being. "Really? You'd want that? Welcome it? It would mean tons of work. I'll pitch in and help, of course."

■ ■ ■

I've never had the chance to feel like a real couple with someone. Sam insisted on shopping with me, particularly when it came to

acquiring the ingredients needed to pull off not one but three parties in close succession. Hand in hand or with his arm wrapped
around my shoulders or waist, we took in the holiday scene.

While at a favorite fondue place, where we sipped cocktails
and dipped sweets in decadent melting pots of gooey goodness, I
shared another secret with Sam.

"Sam, I've been meaning to tell you, but surely you've seen for
yourself…"

He grasps my hand, leaning into me. Concern written all over
his face, he asks, "What is it? Tell me, babe."

"I'm invisible." Sitting back, I wait for his response.

Licking his lips and puckering his brow in confusion, Sam gives
me a questioning look. "Come again?"

"I know you can hear and see me, and better than anyone outside of Aunt Alphia. But really, to most others, I'm invisible. Think
about it."

At that moment, our server returns. "Can I get you anything
else, sir?" she asks sweetly, coyly batting her eyelashes at Sam while
totally ignoring me.

"Yeah, I'll take another one of these," he answers, tapping his
cocktail glass. She gives him another smile. Just as she is about to
hurry away, Sam halts her. "Daria? How about you? Another?"

"Yes, please."

The server frowns.

"The lady will take another as well."

"Sure thing." Server hurries off.

"Bet ya she forgets mine and brings two for you," I say.

"You're on."

It's all I can do to keep from laughing as it plays out.

"You were right," Sam remarks when finally I have the new drink
in hand. It took several attempts to get the server to figure it out.

"Not saying I'm a believer, but you need more than one incident to establish a theory and a principle based in fact."

"You are right," I acknowledge.

■ ■ ■

Sam

"It was like a blind man finally being given the gift of sight. Everywhere we went...Daria was right. How is that?" I exclaim to Joe.

"Give a for instance."

"Okay, try this. We're at the mall, trying to find something for Lucy. We're standing near the second-story balcony railing, looking over the central courtyard decorations. We'd been standing there for a few minutes. Out of nowhere, this lady pushing a stroller, texting, nearly runs right smack into Daria. Would have hit her if I hadn't intervened and stopped the stroller. And all the lady can do is toss me a smile and say, 'Hey, watch it,' to Daria. As if it were her fault."

"The lady was an idiot and too engrossed in her cell. Had to blame someone. The other chick is the easiest target. Doesn't prove your theory, Bro."

"Yeah, what about all those people who nearly mow her over in the grocery store? Huh? Or the server?"

"Hope you didn't give that one a tip." Joe snorts.

"Yeah, I did, one she didn't like, and passed it on to the manager too. Said my tip was to not ignore half of her customer base. I would never have chosen to go into that establishment if it wasn't for Daria. Did so to please Daria and because I trust her when it comes to food. Now I'm reluctant to return because of the server."

"But who *does* see her, I mean, really focuses and sees that darling woman?" Joe asks. "I'd be after that lovely lady, and a few of the boys would, too, if we didn't know that you wanted more than her cookies and pie." He wings his eyebrows suggestively. "Since meeting her, I got me a new appreciation for women of varying sizes. Was a real dick before, thinking that only slim women were hot." He shakes his head. "No more. I want more than the outside package. The inside is what counts."

Yeah, she's met the guys. And I mean more than simply peeping through her blinds alone in her home while we have fun. Been to a few parties. Invited them over and they us. To start, she was real nervous. Has loosened up quite a lot since then. Progress.

"Besides you and the guys…Each time she takes me into one of those specialty food shops, everyone there seems to know her. Eyes light up, smiles brighten. Other customers are hastily dealt with and sent on their way so the focus can be placed on Daria. By extension, I'm accepted. Instantly made part of the club, the family."

"There you go, Bro. It's with the heart that we see rightly. When people use their hearts to focus their vision, Daria is as she has always been and will be…"

"A vision. A person of warmth, love, and passion," I conclude. "For the fools or those confusing what love really is, she's either invisible or not worth their time. Written off."

The world is chock full of fools.

■ ■ ■

I went with Daria to drop off a large tray of holiday cookies to a hospice center. When she was visiting with a few of the staff, one of the nurses took me aside. I learned a lot.

"That Daria. Now, she's someone real special. So don't go playing with her heart. Did you know that the rest of her family hardly bothered with Alphia Rose? When finally Miss Alphia was brought here to us, it was Daria that stayed with her day and night until the last. Even then she was holding her hand, stroking her hair, whispering softly to her, kissing her cheek."

"No, ma'am, I didn't know. I do know she had a deep love for her aunt Alphia. Still does."

"Love doesn't ever die. Some don't know it, but that there girl dropped everything for her aunt."

I tilt my head, an invitation to continue.

"Daria, now, she had a nice job back then, working for a publishing house out of New York City. Paid nice, lots of benefits, with chances of promotion and all. She gave it all up in a snap soon as she heard Miss Alphia was ailing and needing help."

"Was that when she started freelancing as an editor?"

"Uhm-hmm. Had clients by then that wanted her more than the company. The company kept her on retainer for her services. Still does from what I hear. Anyway...Daria wouldn't hear of moving the aunt to a special care center or nursing home, like the family suggested. Besides, it wasn't what Miss Alphia wanted. She wanted to stay in her home, surrounded by her pretties and her garden. Daria sold everything she had and moved in with her aunt. Took care of her and her home and garden. Why, the doctor said it made Miss Alphia live longer than even he expected."

Wow, I hadn't known. It helps more with understanding Daria's family and the dynamics. My woman with the gooey warm center has a spine. She stood upon love and principle, even if it meant standing against those she loves desperately.

"Several times a year, Daria brings in trays of food. Some for the staff. Others for those waiting for the end of life. Food brings so much comfort for those whose hearts are aching. And she knows it."

Chapter 14

Daria

Christmas morning, I lie recovering from my recent, unwrapped orgasmic present, snuggling against Sam. Our bliss is interrupted by the rude chiming of the doorbell.

"Just ignore it." I yawn, snuggling deeper into my man.

Sated and warm, I'm satisfied to linger here awhile before life and living intrude. Sam tucks strands of hair behind my ear. I love these gentle, almost absentminded kisses he places on my head, face, and shoulders. His love-drunk caresses.

"Could be important, Daria. Not everyone comes calling this time of the morning, and it being Christmas," Sam reasons. The hand on my ass that's been gently caressing that flesh squeezes before suddenly slapping.

"Your family will be coming over. Might as well get up and get things going." I concede the inevitable.

Slipping feet into fuzzy-bunny house shoes and my languid body into a pink, puffy robe, I shuffle toward the door, pausing slightly until I'm sure that Sam is behind me. He is. Behind me, beside me, or in front—fast and furiously, I'm getting used to having the man in my life.

As I blink at the absence of any human on the porch, an excited, attention-seeking yip has me looking down. There at my feet, snuggling deep in a blanket, "A puppy!" A baby golden retriever and a silver tabby. "A kitten!"

Letting out gasps of double-dipped delight and surprise, I scoop both up in my arms. All sleepiness has fled. Twirling around, I say, "Sam, someone's left babies on the doorstep."

Hefting the basket, he brings it inside before shutting the door. He waves a hand, apparently at someone passing by. Morning walker, no doubt. A quirky grin is on his face. A devilish twinkle in his eyes.

"Must be a gift from Santa," he remarks as he follows me. I carry both babies into the kitchen, only making it to the hearth rug before plopping down to cuddle and check out the cuties. Now that they are awake and in a warm environment, they've come alive.

I'm giving Sam questioning glances while caught up in the novelty of the babies.

"The...uh...bows around their necks?" he offers.

Hmm.

"Is there a note, some card?" I ask in between kissing the puppy and kitten.

"Looks like love at first sight," Sam comments, coming to join us. "The note says, 'We need a heart and home, someone to call our own.' So what do you think? Gonna keep 'em?"

Longing and love soften my face; my heart is melting. "I've never had a pet before."

"What? Never?"

"Mom wouldn't allow it. Said it was too much trouble and responsibility." Chewing my lower lip, my teeth don't release it until Sam teases it away. "Do you think I am ready? That I can handle it?"

Giving me an are-you-crazy look, he says, "Daria, you can handle anything and everything. Besides, you already own chickens. You mother-hen them as any dotting parent clucks after her chicks. A cat and dog aren't much different except they live in the main house, not a guest cottage out back. The question is, do you want to? Do you want it enough to at least try?"

The exploring babies have stopped. Both give me quizzical expressions. Funny how they so much match Sam's. I giggle deliriously. The puppy barks her approval. The kitten launches herself at me as if overcome with glee.

Quickly, I'm covered in kisses: Holly's, Mistletoe's, and Sam's.

■ ■ ■

Christmas late lunch or early dinner with Sam's family is a success. The puppy and kitten are a success, too, getting so much attention it drives them dizzy, overwhelmed with attention. I end up placing them back in my bedroom with their new beds, also delivered by Santa Sam and smuggled into the house, where the two snuggle together to snooze off their exhaustion.

"Daria, I am amazed each time I encounter you. First your food. Again your food"—BB's words, getting chuckles all around—"now your home. I can't wait to get a tour of your yard and garden when it is green and lush."

We move from the table, each carrying an after-dinner drink into the sitting area. Bellies are full. A fire burns in the hearth, adding to the delicious mellow of the moment. Nothing could make it more perfect.

I snuggle into Sam as he sits in the corner of the leather couch; his arms come around me. In one hand, he holds up a box. "What's this?" I ask. Reflexes have me automatically taking the thing.

Sitting us up, he encourages, "Open it and find out."

A quick glance at his family shows that they've awakened from their catatonic slumber, pulled their attention from the movie on the screen, and are fully alert. Staring at me. Suddenly, my hands are clammy.

Doing as Sam has suggested, I ease the lid open. A ring.

Sam shifts so he is now kneeling at my feet. "For many, this may be sudden. For me, it's a dream come true. When love comes, when love happens, one shouldn't worry about the speed or its timing. It's all in the knowing that truly matters. I knew it the moment I first laid eyes on you. Took my time scoping you out before I made my move. Babe, you're it for me. I love every moment of this," he says, moving a finger between the two of us. "I want more of it. Every day. So if you want it, want me, all I want for Christmas is for you to say yes and agree to be my wife. Daria, will you marry me?"

■ ■ ■

Sam

My woman makes me a happy man. Cheers resound when Daria utters her response. "Yes." Then she bursts into tears. "Happy tears," she explains.

"Must be catching," Matthew murmurs. Mom and Lucy are engulfing Daria and blubbering just the same.

"Let them have their moment, Son," Dad says. "This is one of those special moments in a woman's life. They're simply overcome with joy. All three, and you being the cause." He thumps me on the back.

"And I'm liverwurst?" I mockingly exclaim. "Can't we guys be delirious with joy?"

"Hand me a tissue," Luke simpers, dramatically quivering his lips before throwing himself into my arms.

Pushing him off, I say, "Get off me, you lug. Pull yourself together."

"But I thought you said we of the manly sort should be expressing what it is we feel on the inside." He sniffs, dabbing at his eyes. "I take it that this isn't the moment you've been dreaming of?"

"What, no filling of a hope chest while dreaming of being a groom?" Matthew teases.

"That's all sugar and icing. It's the asking and answering that really counts. All else is just buttercream. That's been done. Accomplished. As far as I'm concerned, we're joined."

I have to blink several times when I see that all have turned to look at me. It takes all my willpower not to rub my nose or mouth, thinking I've some particle stuck there.

Leave it to the mature one in the room to cut the heavy silence. "Can I be a bridesmaid?" Lucy asks excitedly.

"Lucybells, that isn't my decision. Besides, I've just popped the question on my lovely. The rest of how to bring it about is an area I haven't even thought on." As I was alluding to, with no effect, obviously. "For all I know, Daria and I might decide to elope to Vegas…" Mom's horrified gasp has me rethinking that idea.

I look to Daria for help. "Save me," I mouth.

"As my firstborn, I will hunt you down, Sam Bixby, if you even think of marrying this girl in secret. This child has been hidden away far too long. I won't stand for another second of it, and not when it comes to what should be a joyous declaration and celebration of marriage and love."

"Your mom's spoken, Son." Ringing endorsement if ever I heard one from the guy.

"I'm thinking a spring wedding. Maybe here, in your backyard…"

■ ■ ■

This meeting is not going as I expected. Well, what can one assume when it takes until Groundhog Day before we can find a compatible date on which to gather at my place? From the moment Rachel Roth entered my home, her eyes have been glued to Daria's left hand. I don't think she's looked Daria in the eye, let alone said hello.

Shucking her coat, she tossed it to Daria without a blink or thanks, stomping directly to the table and sitting herself down. Daria, the consummate hostess, poured coffee into a traditional coffee service. She even poured each of us a cup, fixing it just the way she knew each liked. An array of finger foods are decoratively arranged for easy access. It's like high tea.

"And how do you think that made me feel? Hearing from others"—a.k.a. Bunny Bixby, my mom—"that my first born daughter was *engaged* and planning her wedding? My own daughter doesn't have the *respect* or *decency* to tell me herself."

Glancing over at Mr. Roth, I see his eyes rolling at his wife's words. A muscle is ticcing in his cheek.

Though Rachel proceeds to fill her plate, she gives Daria's frame a withering look, tsking at what she sees on Daria's plate. As she opens her lips to spew forth some vile remark, I decide I've had enough.

"Bite your tongue or a bit of cucumber sandwich, Mrs. Roth, before you say something that you'll regret or I take greater offense to," I warn.

Amazingly, she shoves the triangle into her mouth, her neck and face a crimson shade at having been called out—and by me.

"This is exactly what we are here to discuss. You are a guest in my home, yet since arriving, you've treated Daria as if she were a doormat and your personal servant. You haven't even bothered to say hello, though you've spewed enough hot air to berate her at every turn and were about to do so again if I hadn't stopped you."

"A mother's observations," she defends the latter, not addressing the former.

"Dear, it's those constant hounding observations and the accumulation of the same and the manner in which you deliver them that are the issue," Mr. Roth interjects. "None doubt you love our Daria. What we question is the manner in which you select to display that motherly love and concern."

Daria turns eyes of amazement and wonder on her father, while I nod my agreement with his words.

"Knowing that Daria would live a life of ridicule, I've done my best to see that she has not," Rachel defends her actions.

"By constantly ridiculing and belittling her at every turn yourself? By being the one who humiliates her, not only at home but in public as well? Beating others to it so that the shame of her weight does not reflect poorly on you for raising a fat daughter?" Mr. Roth states sharply. Okay, seems this is turning into a family therapy session.

"She's fat, David."

"Always have been, Mother. Likely to remain so for the rest of my life."

"It's called genetics," I add.

"Something she inherited. Inherited from your side of the family, I might add." Mr. Roth once again enters the fray. Rachel turns huge, round eyes to him. "Of which there is nothing to be ashamed of."

"Mom, why can't you accept me, all of me, including my weight?"

"Because I love my daughter and don't want her to be the laughingstock—"

"Mom, your way of showing love hurts. You hurt me, have hurt me. You continue to do so, even now. If this is your love, then don't. Hate me. I can't and won't take any more of this sort of love." Turning to me, Daria says, "She either doesn't or won't get it. I can't do this…"

"Do you see what this is doing to Daria?" Mr. Roth says admonishingly to his wife. "Must she endure more from the one who should be her fiercest champion? How did you feel when you were publicly shamed for your attempt to shame Daria on her blog? Try living with that. All. Of. Your. Life. That was administered by strangers, acquaintances, clients, and friends who no longer wish to be associated with you. Add to the mix those that say they love you. Now, how would that make you feel?"

Rachel's eyes are beginning to open wide.

"You want to know why I didn't give you a call to tell you of my recent engagement? I didn't want to hear your disbelief that I'd ever find a good and decent man who wanted to put a ring on it, let alone take me to bed, desiring my body and my hand. Next, I didn't want to hear that there would be no bridal gowns large enough to fit one of my size, let alone that would look good on such a frame. Might as well go to the courthouse or Vegas. That way few people could witness my humiliation."

Crystal tears well up in Mrs. Roth's eyes.

"I want joy to fill each moment while I prepare for my wedding, not shame and humiliation. You will not be invited to any of it if you can't be civil, if you have no joy. No longer will I stand for you destroying what happiness I have."

Mrs. Roth's brow furrows. She stops herself from speaking as she considers, then reconsiders some more. Her face pales upon her realization that Daria is right.

With the dignity of a queen, Daria rises. Clearing her throat, she says, "Until you are able or willing to see beyond my layers of fat that so disgust, appall, and humiliate you, until you are capable of seeing me as more than a blob of fat, capable of nothing more than shoveling food in my maw, then this relationship is at an end. Goodbye, Mother. Thank you for coming. Good day." Daria walks away, slipping out the back door to return to her private sanctuary.

Chapter 15

Daria

Standing behind my VariDesk, another Christmas present from Sam, I notice an all-too-familiar car pulling into Sam's driveway.

Victoria.

Is she lost? Gotten it wrong as to which house is mine? I watch in stunned amazement as she flicks a nasty look in my home's direction before sauntering up the walk to Sam's door on her mile-high high heels, the kind normally seen on pole dancers. Them shoes ain't meant for walking. They are made for...

Straight away, I race to the laundry room that has a window better placed for seeing his entryway. It doesn't take long before Sam's answering the door. I'm even more shocked when Sam gives her entry. He, too, flicks an odd yet hasty look in my direction. During the day, we work from our separate offices. Mine here. His there. We've tried several variations. None have worked. In each attempt, we've found ourselves naked on the floor or on a table or whatever flat or not-so-flat surface is handy.

What business would he have with Victoria, or she with him? None of my business? Big rock candy mountain! I'm making it my business.

Like a suffragette or a prohibitionist of old, I march smartly over to Sam's, selecting the back door as my point of entry. The door reserved for friends, family, and fiancée. I decide to go in commando style, not ninja warrior or stealth 007 mode. Pushing into the room as if I've come to borrow a cup of sugar, all neighborly like, I then come to a NASCAR stop.

And what before my eyes should appear? Why, a red-faced Sam and Victoria's bared rear—along with the rest of her. Naked. In Sam's house. Naked. Standing in front of my man. Naked. Puddled at her feet is her coat. She was naked underneath her faux-fur coat. Naked. Still is. Standing in nothing but those fuck-me shoes, of which I bet Clarise has a pair, along with several additional options.

And what do I say?

"Interesting tattoo, Victoria. Does Mom know about it?"

That has her jumping in startled surprise, whirling around to confront. How do I know? Her hands. They don't attempt to cover—anything. They're fisted. Knuckles are turning white.

"Ah, Daria. Sneaking around? What, not enough food at your place that you have to pillage your neighbors for scraps?" she sneers.

"With this figure? Do you think I settle for just scraps?" I titter, fake laughter ringing as hollow as it's intended. "If it isn't quality, I might chew, but I rarely swallow." Sam likes that one. "Since you know, already copped to knowing, that I live next door, can I assume that you being here *isn't* a mistake? Are you lost? Or have you simply lost your French-fried mind?" I say, crossing my arms and giving her my best "for shame" look.

"My reasons for being here are none of your business," she hisses heatedly.

When she directs her bedroom eyes on Sam, he wisely raises his hands and backs up before circling around behind me. Being the man he is, he doesn't remain there long, choosing to step out to the side but remain nearest to me. My man.

"Disagree. Unless the master of the house says otherwise, I'm making it my business," I say, turning to include a rather stunned Sam. "Sam?"

In his momentary stunned silence, Victoria triumphantly shakes her honey-blonde hair so it cascades down her naked back. Her perky breasts jut out, as if they are heat-seeking missiles that have located their target. Sam. The deadly cat grin appears on her youthful face, making her wide mouth wider.

"Why, Daria," she purrs maniacally, "didn't you know? I have a standing appointment with Sam here. Come by routinely for a little afternoon delight. A little nooky cookie."

Tilting my head, I scornfully say, "Victoria, I've known for some time now that you're a bitch. When did you become a whore? If you're needing cash so badly, why not hit up Dad for an increase in your allowance?" I hold up my hand as anger boils up in Victoria. "And before you explode, know this. Sam is not that kind of man. He doesn't pay for sex. Doesn't need to. Would never do so. As for sneaking around and having affairs…Now, that's not his style either. Don't know what trick you're trying to pull, but there will be no payout today. At least what you're expecting to get. Sam is not your john."

"Sam and I have been seeing each other since the night of the dinner, when you embarrassed me, trying to steal *my* chosen man away."

I laugh at her words. That has Victoria blinking.

"Are you on something, or are you just stupidly delusional?" I turn to Sam, who has strangely allowed me to dominate this scene. "Sam, what have you to say? Been skipping through the tulips, doing the horizontal tango with this whorey Tory?"

Desperately, he tries swallowing his mirth. "Victoria, I may be the man in your imagination, maybe of your dreams. When it comes to reality, I've already selected my life's mate. Victoria, it isn't you."

"Wh-what?" She gives a self-sweep of her hand from her head down to her toes, then sweeps me with the same, as if to compare.

Seriously? She's shocked? Stunned? Surprised? Where are the tears? If she were in love, having a real romantic tryst, where is the anger? The sorrow? Just fabricated dismay. Why?

"Victoria, so your head and whatever is rattling around inside pulls it together, there has never been anything between us." Finger volleying between him and her. "There is lots going on between me and Daria." He picks up my hand and kisses my wrist, then my cheek. "This is the first time and the last time I will see you unclothed and naked in my home." Stern voice. "I will not tolerate your scheming machinations to undermine Daria's happiness. I will not be a tool to be used that way. What you do here today cheapens you, is disrespectful toward me, and is mean-spirited at best toward your sister, Daria."

He pauses, giving Victoria time to let his words sink in. We might be waiting until the rapture...

"The fact that Daria does not question my integrity next to your scheming says wonders about her. Further proof that I have chosen well." God, I love this man!

Victoria gives him a confused look. She is slow to realize that her plan has backfired and her naked pussy is on full display. Is that Joe peeking in through the window? His wide grin follows his glued, wide-eyed stare. Must be close to noon; Joe usually comes by at lunch time to meet and confer as business partners with Sam. Further proof that Victoria is lying.

"Victoria, you are physically pretty. No denying that fact. I and all who look can see your outer beauty. Seeing too much of it at the moment." He mutters that last bit. "That is not in question here. It's your inner self that's repellent to me. Has been since that dinner." That has her recoiling. "You took every opportunity to put down, humiliate, and push aside your sister. In order to make yourself look good, you threw dirt at another. Not cool, Victoria. Not cool at all. Even my brothers noticed. Mark my words. Your body might attract men, but any man who truly is an honorable one at heart won't stay around long. You gotta change your heart, your soul. Those are what keep a man once he's found his way to your door."

Facing me, Victoria remains furiously persistent. "Sam's lying. We've been having an affair. In fact...I'm pregnant." Flipping a glance at Sam, she bites her lower lip and clutches her hands together. "I didn't want to inform you this way..." Delicate white hands press to her lower belly.

If Victoria is pregnant with Sam's baby, then I'm the Queen of Sheba. Unless.

"Have you ever donated semen?" I ask, narrowing my eyes and furrowing my brow.

Sam chuckles his response.

"Stop the sausage-link drop, sis. You're no more pregnant than Mom. I'm not sure what game you're playing at, but clearly Sam and I are not on board. In fact, dear Sister, you have long worn out your welcome. I insist that you leave. Take your deceitful ass and your lying, plucked pussy elsewhere."

With a firm grasp on her arm, I help her on her walk of shame. That's right. I march her jiggly naked butt out of the house, escorting her to her car. Each step farther into the natural light of the out-of-doors and the full light of day has her struggles increasing. Mounting resistance results in an ever-firmer grip on her arm, until I am dragging her.

"What are you doing?" she hisses. "Don't you see I'm naked?" Her mortified squeals make me giggle.

"Not completely, Sister. You've still got on your fuck-me shoes. But it was the look you were going for, after all. Thought you might want others besides Sam and myself to see all of your... ass-ets. Free advertising. Who knows, you might find a willing customer. As for Sam...So sorry it didn't work the way you wanted. Good luck with the next sucker. Might want to bring knee-padding for that."

To my delight, a sizable number of neighbors are happening by, including Mable and her afternoon ladies that walk the neighborhood. Hmm. Seems today is walking-with-the-hubby day too. Co-ed retirees out for a stroll. How nice.

"Hi, ladies. Gentlemen. Neighbors and their friends," I say, waving cheerfully.

Victoria's audible inhalation only makes my giggle turn into all-out, cackling laughter.

Sam's following behind, carrying her coat. And her keys. I take them from him, deliberately fumbling with the keys. Taking several times to hit the fob juuust right. Darn that help button. The loud sound of the car alarm has others coming to their windows. How nice knowing that there are caring people willing to come to see just what all the fuss is about. The manufactured delay increases naked exposure time, increasing shame and humiliation. A harsh lesson, but hopefully one mastered.

"There a problem, Daria?" Mable asks cheekily.

"No, just a special delivery misdirected." I chortle. "Just helping this lost soul find the light and the naked truth of it all."

Finally, Victoria's pinkening, heart-shaped ass is planted in her winter-chilled seat. I take further satisfaction in seeing the goosflesh rising on her skin. I've tossed her coat way in the back.

Yeah, mean, but hey, what's a sister to do under the circumstances? What's shocking is that Victoria is willing to call me out on it.

"Daria, that was spiteful and mean, and you know it," she bites.

I crook a brow. "No, that was added payback. Mean would be to toss you out on your very bare pussy and very bare, naked ass and not have given you your coat, or these?" I dangle the keys before her shocked face, wiggling them like a pendulum. Hypnotic. Amusement flares as I watch her eyes following the movement. She licks her lips. She jumps, attempting to snag them when I pretend to toss them away. Folding them in my hand, I wait until she meets my hardened eyes.

Finally, she sees my wrath, along with my disappointment. There is sorrow too.

"Whatever my trespasses are that have so thoroughly infested you with such vile hate, I am truly sorry. Even more so that I haven't a clue as to what that may be. I wish with all my heart that you would have chosen to speak to me about your feelings in a mature manner, the way two adults and loving sisters should. That was not to be. Pity." Hopefully, she sees the truth of my words.

Her lower lip trembles. She grits her teeth.

"To come between me and my man"—I flip my hand so she can see the ring that gleams there, circling my finger—"in such a manner…" I heave a pain-filled sigh. "You've gone too far this time." With tears in my eyes, I tell her, "You're dead to me."

Wide-open, rounded eyes stare back at me. A startled look with oh-lips. My words have sunk in. Victoria's face crumbles. I stick the key in her ignition, turn my back, and walk away. I don't look back. Not when the car's engine starts or when I hear it back up and drive away.

"Did you hear the siren?" Sam hurries in a few minutes later.

Tearfully, I nod.

"It was Victoria." Sam catches me as I attempt to race past to see if she's okay. "Relax, the cop that patrols the area was sitting just beyond the community entrance. Pulled her over. Ticketed her for indecency. Driving while naked."

"Didn't even have the smarts to pull over and get her coat," I mutter with a shake of my head.

Sam gathers me in his arms. There, held safe and loved in his strong, warm cocoon, I weep. In so many weeks, I've lost two family members. There is no doubt I may lose more.

Chapter 16

Daria

"The boys are coming over tonight," Sam informs me. Once every other week, Sam and his bike buddies get together, mixing it up where they meet. It's sort of a rotation. What they do, I haven't a clue. Sam won't say.

Tossing back a few is a certainty. Playing cards? Pool? I've asked, more than once, and all I get is an awkward sort of stilted silence. A strange gurgling emanates from his throat before he clamps it tight shut. It's the blush that gets my notice. That doesn't do anything to squelch my curiosity. It does the opposite. So I have me a plan.

"Where are you gonna have it?"

"Can we use your lower level? The guys like the downstairs wine cellar..."

Uhm-hmm. They like the kegs on tap as well, and any batch of the distilled stuff I might have barreled and ready for sipping.

"Gonna need some snacks and stuff?" I offer. It never fails to shock me, seeing the look of delight that shines from his beautiful face. This man of mine rocks me every time.

He shrugs. "Don't want to put you out, babe. Thought I'd pick up some crackers and spread, sliced summer sausage, and chips and dip, call it a feed."

"Well, if you'd rather that," I reply, returning the shrug, "have at it. Just thought…"

Perking up and falling for the bait, he asks, "Thought what? Do you have any other ideas? Suggestions? You know the crew that's coming over. They'd eat about anything you shove in front of them. Of course, you'd have a sizable group of guys to fill out scorecards if you want to try out a new recipe with variations. Kind of like guinea pigs for your blog." He thinks he's sooo cute. Thing is…he is.

"I'll take care of it, sweetie. Can't have my guy handing out chips and dip and leave it at that." Loud, wet, smoochy smooches have me giggling.

"You're the best, babe."

"Uh-huh. I like hearing it." An idea strikes. "If you bucks are having your male-bonding soiree, can I have a doe party?"

"Huh?"

"Well, I'm not asking for permission, only if you would object and how strong—"

His finger placed upon my lips cuts off my words.

"Let me get this straight, my introverted woman wants to have people over? People that *you've* invited for a party of your own?"

"Yeah, got a problem with that?" I taunt mockingly, hands on hips, giving him what I think is a tough-gal look.

"*Grrrlol,*" Sam exclaims, seizing me by my hips and pulling me into him. Playfully, he chomps his teeth before grazing them along my neck. I tilt my head, giving him greater access. Those magical lips of his find their way to my own, plundering them in a way that makes me forget everything but him and me and us.

"Who do you plan on inviting?" he asks between nuzzles, nibbles, and kiss-pops.

Since we've started living together and come out as engaged, I've managed to meet several of the ladies that are paired with some of Sam's motorcycle friends. Most have been welcoming. A few have become friends. I want to encourage that budding friendship to grow.

"Our two groups don't have to mingle. Separate floors or even separate houses. Since whatever you boys do is so sacred and secret, we ladies will leave you to it and have our own fun."

■ ■ ■

"Killer idea, Daria. Glad you came up with it. Inviting a few of us over and all. Wasn't looking forward to a night by my lonesome," Paige admits while petting Holly and Mistletoe, who have been vying for her attention.

"I got to thinking, the guys are doing their thing…Why not us?"

"I like how your mind works, bella," Stephanie says, coming to join us.

So, too, do Nina and Karen. They've been scoping out the house, again.

"So what's on the agenda?" Karen asks, nibbling on some finger foods I placed out.

"Movies? Consumption of alcohol and eating?" Stephanie throws out.

"Uhm-hmm, if you like," I agree, sloshing the first round of strawberry daiquiris into glasses that are eagerly accepted.

"How about going for a dip in that pool of a tub?" Karen suggests, gulping a bit after the idea hits in midsip. She scoops up a wad of napkins to dab up the pink liquid that's spilled on her blouse.

"Fill us in on wedding plans. Hey, is that a devilish look on your face I see?" Paige asks, setting down her drink and giving me a considering look. "You already have an idea. Spill it."

"Well, for starters…" My cheeks are turning crimson. "I'm rather curious as to what the guys are up to. I want to know what it is the guys are doing in secret. Any of you know?"

"No, but we can find out," Paige says, popping a small finger quiche into her mouth, giving us a devious smile while chewing.

"How?"

"Didn't Sam set up a security system?"

"Yeah. Yeah! I think I might know what you're suggesting…"

"We can use your office computer and simply use the lower-level monitoring devices to see what they're doing."

"Eye-in-the-sky—or in the house—sort of scenario… Brilliant."

Like preteens at a sleepover, we giggle as we rush back to my office. Drinks in hand, each one snags a food plate. After I key into my computer, Paige takes over. "Be my guest," I say wryly.

We all huddle around, watching.

I shake my head in bemusement. "Nah, can't be. Can it?"

"Seriously? This is what they've been doing? Keeping secret all this time?" Nina snorts.

"I mean…I expected they might be playing cards, or working on some bike, but…this?" Nina gestures toward the monitor.

"The evidence is there. Right here before our eyes…" Stephanie shakes her head in disbelief.

"They're holding a…"

"Book club discussion group." True enough, our tough, manly-man, badass guys are engaged in sharing their perspectives on a recent read.

"That explains it," Stephanie says in a stunned voice. Registering our stares, she elaborates, "My missing books. Several times, my books have gone missing, or I find them where I *know* I didn't leave them."

"Wh…What sort of books?" Paige asks, clearly bewildered.

"Romance."

Say what? We giggle at the notion.

"Let's get the sound. Hear what they're saying," I say after shaking away the zombie moment of shock.

"Were you hooked or intrigued by the way the book started?" Keevan, Stephanie's guy, asks. I elbow her. We both share a look and smirk. "I mean, like, is it believable? A chick heaving a backpack over one shoulder is standing in the middle of an intersection of two major rural roads…"

"She's got to decide the direction her life will take."

"Life is a journey. So many paths. So many directions. Endless possibilities. Same as the flat prairie or endless acres of corn and wheat stretched out seemingly without end."

"Yeah, but the wind? She decides because the wind seems to tug and push her in one direction…"

"Fate. Destiny. Trusting in forces beyond our scope of understanding. True surrender…"

Discussion ensues.

We ladies share grins at the depth of sharing our guys are engaged in.

"Sexy as all get out." Karen grins. "My big, lovable teddy bear…"

We all laugh and groan.

"What book are they discussing?" Nina asks.

"Yeah, Paige, can you zoom in to catch a cover or any indication as to which book they're reading?"

Paige does just that.

A gasp has us all turning to Karen. "OMG. It's really a romance novel. I know this book. No wonder I couldn't find my copy. He swiped it. It's a contemporary, with elements of suspense."

Our attention is momentarily diverted when the next discussion question is offered up.

"What is your favorite quote or part in the story?"

The passages they share tell me all I need to know. "*The Road Leading Home*. Author, Sonsy Falstaff," I mutter.

"You know? I've seen other works of hers lying around our place. Dog-eared pages. Some pages even have Post-its. Did a quick flip through and found passages highlighted. Not just the sex passages, but others as well. Like, he's got this color-coding system…" Stephanie shakes her head. "Asked him about it too. Keevan just shrugged it off, saying the book must belong to his sister. Took it right out of my hands, mumbling something about how he'd get it back to her and all. All this time…"

"Wait a sec. Are they *embarrassed*…by others figuring out what, exactly?" My earlier amusement gives way to a bit of pique.

"Embarrassed at being caught reading? In a book club of biking bros?"

"Or reading romance?"

"How about all three?" Yeah, that sounds like the way of it.

"Lots of commercial fiction is in fact romance without the label. They disguise it by having the story male-centered and with more action. All have a hero and a heroine. There's attraction, conflict, and resolution with a happily ever after. Look at all the popular movies that come out of books. Following essentially the same formula as a romance. Guys would drop dead if they realized most are repackaged romances."

"Well, what do we do now? Now that we know?" Karen asks what we each have been asking in our heads.

"Ah, let them have their secret. Now we know what to get them for presents and birthdays and such."

Milewide grins and twinkling eyes are exchanged among us. Mine falters when I hear the next words.

"Daria has set out on her own metamorphosis. A new journey. Like this main character, Daria, too, has known joy and sorrow. Both have left their marks, profoundly influencing her and how she interacts with the world. Both have influenced who and what she is now. However, I firmly believe that events don't make the person. They might help to hone or hinder, but the person she is, is the person she was and will always be. She would be herself at her core regardless of her upbringing. In the end, our life's journey is one that leads us home. One where we learn not only who and what we are but accept the answer. In time, we all should come to value and love ourselves, warts and all." Tilting his head, he ponders. "I think soul recognizes soul…"

"And her ass," Joe says.

Flames of red flood my face with those words. My new friends giggle.

"True. The gravity of her luscious full moon pulled me in. Believe me, I went willingly. Now I never want to leave her orbit. She's it for me, man." A wistful, dreamy expression illuminates Sam's face, until Joe elbows him into awareness.

"Stop bragging, Bro. That is one secret treasure, that one. What with her talents, cooking…" Joe licks his chops. "A guy would be stupid to overlook her."

"But that's it. So many have, on account…"

"Of her weight? Her size?" Heads nodding around.

"Weight, body-shape, like hair color, may be a particular preference for some, but if it's the only characteristic that one uses to separate chaff from the wheat, then most suckers would starve. Got to be open to love no matter its shape, color, texture, or form."

"Size is relative," Foster says, gaining everyone's attention. "Take my Nina, for instance." We all look her way, noting her facial expression and body language. "She's no Barbie doll, and thank God for it. She's been complaining about some extra twenty pounds she's put on that seem stuck in her ass and hips. Near drives me crazy. I love those pounds on her. They sit just right. Fit perfectly when I pull her back at night, snuggling her close…"

I hand her a tissue.

We each are amazed by the things the guys share about their partners.

"Daria has been trained to hate her shell. I wish, in time, she'll learn to love herself the way I love her. See her beauty the way I do. Only when she loves her body will she find that the cloak of invisibility she believes engulfs her will finally fall away, or it will cease to matter."

"I love this guy!" I say from the depths of my soul.

Chapter 17

Daria

With the coming of the new season, Sam and I, along with Holly and Mistletoe, enter into a new routine as a family. For all practical purposes, Sam and I are living together.

We rise from bed together. After coffee and breakfast, I walk Holly *and* Mistletoe. The cat will not be left behind. Sam sometimes comes with; usually the girls and I walk him to his office, then go off on our way. Having both a young dog and cat on leashes is a situation that gets curious double takes, along with the occasional comment.

Being out in the full light of day, lapping the neighborhood with poop bags in hand, no longer seems an impossible or apprehensive task. It's wondrous seeing the world change around me as we take our morning stroll. Bulbs are emerging, buds gearing up to burst forth with flower and leaf. The greening of the grass. The earth is warming, leaving its foggy breath in the mornings.

The beauty and tranquility of the moment is lost when a white SUV comes flying around the curve. Sonic speed achieved. I shake my head. Some things never seem to change. It's that platinum blonde again. On her phone. Again. Apparently, she doesn't see me. Nothing new. Still invisible to some, I guess.

The timing of it all couldn't have been planned any better. The speed demon overshoots the turn, ignoring the stop sign as always, at the same time my foot descends from the curb. The laws of motion and inertia being what they are mean that two bodies are bound to collide.

Holly lets out a barking alarm. Mistletoe is in total agreement. With a simple yank, she's freed herself from my hold, doing a series of rapid gazelle leaps, keeping on the tail of her canine sister. A split second after realizing my babies have reached a point of safety, I feel myself going airborne. This is no elegant flight of a swan, with pinwheeling arms and flailing wildly about in those few seconds that seem like centuries. In that time frame, a second vehicle comes flying from another direction, knocking me like a ping-pong ball.

As it rams into me, I'm sent flying in some bizarre aerial performance, where I splat flat like a giant squashed bug before rolling up and over the windshield, which shatters into a weblike pattern from the force and weight of the impact, and then I tumble to the ground.

Vaguely aware of a fuzzy, weighted purr along my jugular. Mistletoe. Holly has come to my rescue as well. Whining, she touches the moist, cold tip of her nose to my cheek, then sets up a neighborhood alert, issuing an unending series of sharp barks.

All goes black.

■ ■ ■

Sam

I love my life. The last several months have been the ultimate. Now that my lady has agreed to marry me, nothing could be more grand. It's as if the planets have all aligned since I made the decision to return to the place of my birth.

Setting up my business. Purchasing a house. Finding Daria. Landing Daria after spying on her for nearly a year...My reverie is abruptly halted when I hear Holly's serial barking penetrating through the layers of windows and walls of my home office. This is not her happy bark.

I find myself running toward the sound. Mom always said that a parent and a lover have an innate sense when something is wrong or out of whack. My instincts are right. Up ahead I see the whirling red and blue lights of the police and the box shape of an ambulance. Mable is hurrying in my direction. When she sees me, her face falls with relief. Frantically, she waves me onward.

"Hurry, Sam! It's Daria."

I pick up the pace, until I feel as if I am a jet on two legs.

"No!" I yell, gasping with soul-wrenching dread when I see Daria being loaded onto a gurney.

I would fall to my knees, but my need to see Daria propels me those last few yards. That bit of distance holds a barrage of storytelling clues. A tragedy. A horror.

"What happened?" I huff, my breathiness more a product of my fear than from exertion. My legs are weak. Wobbling. I'm not sure if I can remain standing for long.

"Do you know her?" A police officer steps between me and my woman, keeping me from her.

"She's my fiancée." I say, trying to shoulder past the officer. He won't allow it.

"Yo, Officer. At least let him take this infernal cat. The darn thing won't release its claw-hold on the woman. Keeps hissing and growling when I try to pick it up."

Taking that as an invitation, I push past the officer. Reaching in, I extract Mistletoe. The only time I get a glimpse of my Daria.

Eyes closed. Neck and head in a brace. Blood drips from nose and mouth. I can already see swelling and a rapid discoloration on one side of her face. Body board. They fear a spinal injury of sorts. Damaged. Hurt.

"Daria! Daria?" I get no response. "I'm here, babe. I won't be far. Hang on, babe. Hang on for me. For us," I call out to her. Gotta stay strong. For her.

I feel a tug on my shoulder pulling me back. "She's unconscious, sir. We're taking her to the ER."

I nod, moving back farther still, though it kills me to do so, in order to let them do their job.

Turning to the officer, I ask, "What happened?"

"The lady—"

"Daria Roth."

"Daria Roth got hit by two separate vehicles," he says, gesturing to the scene.

"I swear. She came out of nowhere," the blonde Bronco bitch whines. "Like a ghost. Invisible."

"She's wearing a fluorescent pink sweatshirt, and you say you didn't see her?" an officer demands.

I can't remain silent. "And I suppose your nose wasn't glued to your cell? That you weren't speeding? Adhering to all rules of the road, including the stop sign?" I rant, gesturing to that visible invisible sign. The one that has the word STOP clearly displayed.

Her brows furrow in confusion. She blinks in puzzlement.

The look disgusts me. "Officer, this lady is known for her excessive speed through here, as she is for distracted driving and her inability to stop. I have a home security system that will show proof of my words when she passes in front of my house and

Daria's home. The HOA has been notified by many in our subdivision. There have been other close calls. We've got many retirees and stay-at-home parents that walk this area, walking with children and pets. She's a menace."

"And I can testify to what Sam Bixby is saying. I saw it with my own two eyes. Was at the window when the entire thing happened…"

Though I'm pleased others are standing up for justice and righteousness, the voices are like droning noises. I need to be with Daria.

The other driver—a kid. The music is still blaring from his car. He has earphones plugged into his ears as well. Why? He sits there on the curb in a daze. Why isn't he in school? It's fucking Tuesday. As if he can sense my gaze, his eyes move to me. Vacant. Can't feel sorry for him just now.

"Was it worth it?" I demand. "Knowing that you hurt a lady, my lady, today because of your stupidity?"

"I was gonna be tardy. Can't be tardy again. I'll get a detention, a call home. Mom and Dad will be pissed. Said they'd take away my keys. Have to take the bus. Now look at it," he whines, gesturing to his car.

My gaze travels over to his banged-up, smashed metal illusion of freedom. I can't help grimacing. Windshield is busted. I can see where Daria made impact. Her blood remains smeared on the glass and metal. I follow the trail to the ground. More blood has pooled, seeping into the pavement. The impact knocked her clear out of a shoe.

"Yeah? And your need to rush and act irresponsibly may have cost someone their life. How are you gonna live with that? Think that will please your folks any more than a fucking tardy? Hey, here's a tip. Wake up earlier. Use two alarm clocks if you have to.

Get out of your fucking bed earlier. Get your lazy ass to school earlier, instead of staying up until three in the morning playing video games." The kid has me riled.

There he sits, not a hair out of place on his greasy, punk head. Sporting the latest in grunge wear. Worrying about his own ass. Does he even mention Daria? Is he the slightest bit concerned for her welfare?

"Just think what it did to my lady, kid. Think about what she's gonna have to endure if she survives—" I bite my own tongue. Refusing to go there. Can't and won't go there.

"Mable?"

"Sam, I'll take Kissy Kitty, and Holly too. Don't you fret. Go be with Daria. The officers will know where to find you if there's a need."

The officer nods. That's my cue to run back home and get my shit together. Gotta pull it together.

■ ■ ■

It takes all I've got to not make the same mistakes as that blonde bitch and the stupid-ass kid involved with putting hurt on my Daria. I wait until I'm in the waiting room before making phone calls.

Hands are shaking. This isn't the news I really want to deliver. Should be more in the lines of, "Congrats, you're grandparents." But it's not. It's worse. "Mr. Roth…"

That's now done, with assurances he'll inform the rest of the Roth family and come ASAP. I place the next call.

"Dad?" I say, attempting to swallow the lump in my throat.

"Son!" Daddar is just as potent as Momdar. His one spoken word is enough to make me crumble, blubbering my reason for the call.

Relief fills me when he assures me he's on the way. "Stay strong, Son. We're on our way. Out the door. We're coming, Son."

"Joe," I begin on my next call, using my thumb to wipe away the sob snot and the lingering tears. There are so many that I end up needing the flat of my hand. "Ahh," I say, clearing my throat, "I need you to get to my house. Key yourself in. Check this morning's security feed. See if you can find a speeding white SUV…"

"Got it, man. Hang in there, Bro. Daria's got grit. She's a fighter. I'll pass the word…"

"Thanks, man." I hang up.

Just in time. The doctor has arrived.

"Mr. Bixby?"

"That's me. Can you tell me how my fiancée, Daria Roth, is?"

His grimace and grim countenance make my belly cramp. So much so, I use my hand to cover my rolled, clamped lips to prevent myself from hurling on his shoes.

"We'll be admitting Ms. Roth. I want to keep her for a few days to monitor her condition. Depending on what we find, her stay may be long. We still have to finish tests and scans. Each takes time. I just wanted you to hear that we've got a team of people making sure she pulls through and that we know of all her injuries, so they can be addressed and treated."

"How badly is she hurt? What can you tell me? They wouldn't let me near her…"

"Concussion, contusions…lots of those. She'll be pretty black and blue for a while. It's the spinal and head injury that has us most concerned. That and possible internal bleeding. We're afraid of brain swelling. The scans will tell us if there is more."

"Swelling of the brain?" A female gasp at the door has the doctor and me turning. Mr. and Mrs. Roth have arrived, along with Braden. Just behind them—my parents.

Quick introductions are made. "Doctor, you were saying… swelling of the brain?"

"It's something we will be watching for. I don't want to borrow trouble. She's going to be in considerable pain when she wakes. She's suffered a broken arm. Lucky is what she is." He shakes his head in disbelief, meaning odds shouldn't be in her favor. "Someone was looking out for her. Trust me, I've seen *a lot* worse on people who seemed barely bumped, lost a bit of skin—road rash—who didn't make it. It's still a possibility. We'll know more about if there are any other injuries after she wakes and as things begin to heal and the swelling decreases."

Questions are asked and answered. "I'll have a nurse inform you once she's been moved to a room or as things develop."

As soon as he's left, everyone circles around me, seeking more information. I tell them what I can. That's when the police officer walks in. He surveys the room, taking note of all who are here.

"Officer," I call out to the man in blue, maneuvering my way through the throng of those who have gathered around me.

"Mr. Bixby, are these people important to Ms. Roth?"

Again, I make introductions.

"We've processed the scene, removed the damaged vehicles. Your business partner, Joe Manning, was very helpful, providing us with feed from the recording of the white SUV. Got similar recordings of the kid. A door-to-door revealed your observation to be accurate. Both have a record of reckless driving. Both have been cited, along with a few other violations. That's on record. Our report will state that Ms. Roth had the legal right of way and was not at fault, placing blame for any and all injuries and damages to any and all parties on the shoulders of the two drivers."

"Meaning that Daria will have to personally sue the two lugheads in order to be compensated for the cost of her medical care, loss of income, et cetera," Dad says, clamping a hand down on my shoulder. "Not a problem. We can arrange that. Got one of the finest attorneys specializing in such cases in the office." Dad is an attorney.

I melt into his arms. He never releases me until I signal to do so.

"Thanks, Dad. All the same, what I want is to see Daria and get her home."

■ ■ ■

What ensues is me keeping an endless vigil.

Day and night I stay by Daria's side. Holding her hand, whispering words to her, kissing her bandaged head and raw, scraped cheeks. The nurses know enough to know that asking me to leave after visiting hours are over is not gonna fly. I'm staying.

Daria falls into a coma.

"Not atypical in such cases. Often we place patients in a medically induced coma to allow them time to heal with less noticeable pain. Daria suffered a severe head injury. May have suffered a stroke. Time will tell. Once the swelling reduces around her brain, we may see her gradually awaken," the doctor says.

"Son, you got to go home. Get some sleep, bathe, put on clean clothing, eat. You have a business to tend to..." Dad places his hand on my shoulder to further gain my attention.

"I can't leave her, Dad."

"Your mom and I will stay until you get back," he tells me. "Has any of her family been here?"

"Mr. Roth comes by every day. Daria's mother..." I shake my head.

Dad sighs heavily. "Go, Son. Daria will want you to take care of yourself..."

That gets me moving. Like a zombie, I take myself home. I'm not in the door five minutes before Mable is there. I close my eyes, wishing the kind lady would go away.

"I'm not going to take up your time, Sam. Holly and Mistletoe can stay with me," she tells me after I give her an update.

My home is too empty, so I go over to Daria's. It's in her bed that I take my ease, finding some comfort with her scent surrounding me and the memory of our times spent together here. Blessed sleep comes. I sleep like the dead. It isn't until late the next day that I awaken to someone pounding at the door.

Rubbing my hands through my rumpled hair, I head toward the door. Don't even bother stripping off my clothing. Looks like I've been sleeping in them for days. Harsh laugh. I've been in them for over five days now. Dad was right. I do need a shower. I stink.

With an angry flourish, I open the front door. Standing before me is a man I know who lives in the neighborhood.

"Sam Bixby, I'm Arthur Collins. Nicholas is my son. He's one of the people who hit Daria Roth. I knew you were home. Wanted to extend my apologies and willingness to do what's right by Ms. Roth." He hands me a business card. "This is how you can contact me. Got the name of my insurance agent and attorney written on the back," he points out. "Call either. Just wanted to extend my apologies and convey my willingness to cooperate. As for Nicholas, he has lost all driving privileges, beyond what the law will require. He is grounded and won't be seeing the light of day unless he's in school or doing his community service work."

I allow the man to drone on. Glad I am there are people who live a principled life.

He leaves with the vow that Daria will be in their prayers. I shower in Daria's watery oasis. It, too, has the ability to soothe some deeper parts of my inner core. With fresh garments on my back, a cup of coffee in hand, and the other holding a toasted ba-gel and shmear, I head back to Daria's office.

First order of business, check my calendar and emails, touch base with Joe. "I got this, Bro. Go do what you need to do for Daria. Spend time with her…" Yeah, I hear the implied meaning. Don't know how much more time I may have with my lady love. Luck may be a fickle lady, but time can be one hell of a bitch.

"I took the liberty of contacting those that needed it, wiping your slate clean," Joe tells me. "I can look after the business until things smooth out for you and your lady."

God, I love my friends. Their support and willingness to take on my load says they, too, value Daria. They accept her and our relationship.

Next I hack into Daria's blog, posting a quick message about Daria, asking for their understanding and their prayers. Also asking that they post thoughts and recollections of their favorite dish and who prepared it. Sort of an ode to those that feed our hearts and souls as well as our bellies, satisfying our taste buds. I'm thinking that Daria would enjoy such entries. They could be something I could read to her.

My plans are to go through her mail and pay any pending bills, then do the same for myself before packing a duffel bag, along with my laptop, which will allow me to work from Daria's hospital room. The stillness of the room has me pausing. Daria's scent lin-gers, as if a part of her soul resides within, though her body is no longer here. Realizing that it is she that gives this place life. Daria's energy buzzes around the place. I find myself roaming the room. I've been here but never took the time to linger and look. I do that now.

Treasures from her travels are displayed in cases, hung from walls, and placed neatly on shelves, all reminding me to call a housekeeping agency to keep things pristine and clean. Daria would like that, and it will relieve another burden. I find myself in front of a bookcase containing shiny new, never-been-read novels. Romances. Multiple copies, all authored by Sonsy Falstaff.

To my amazement, there are five different novels by Falstaff. Daria has the latest one, the one yet to be released. Excitement has me swiping it off the shelf. Turning in my eagerness to sit and read in the hope it will settle and calm my nerves, I then notice a stack of them sitting on her large conference table. A quill-style pen and an old-fashioned blotter sit nearby. I give a quick count. The number equals the members in my book club. Curious.

Replacing the novel on the shelf, I exchange it for one on the table. On the first page is an elegantly written inscription. It reads:

Dearest Sam,
You are the one who truly sees me. Me. It is you that has encouraged me to come out into the light and enter a world from which I've sought so long to hide. Solitude was never the answer. I realize that now. Only in facing the dragon of our fears and torment can we truly see those shackles ease, release, and finally turn to dust. Your love was the key that set me free. Your Daria is spreading her wings. Learning to fly and fly without her safety net, though she knows without a doubt you will always be there to catch her should she falter or flounder. For this, I shall always be truly grateful. Truly, my heart and soul have found its home. They are by your side. Forever.
    Sonsy Falstaff

I know this handwriting. It's the same as Daria's. My Daria. Sonsy more than knows Daria, is friends with Daria. Sonsy *is* Daria. They are one and the same.

Weakened knees have me abruptly sitting. Still stunned, with trembling hands, I flip through a few more covers, searching out the inscription. Each one is made out to one of my brothers who are part of our rogue book club. To each, she's taken the time to personalize a copy.

Staggered.

My lady love has managed to surprise me beyond pride and pleasure. Unashamed, I weep. Weeping for my good fortune in finding such a person to call my own. Weeping for my sorrow that she is not here. Rejoicing that my Daria is truly a phoenix rising. Vowing I will be by her side to see her transform yet again. Once again, I am thunderstruck, astonished, and amazed and so incredibly proud.

I thought to sleep here tonight and return to Daria early tomorrow morning. No longer. With the new book in hand, I grab up my duffel and head to where I belong—at Daria's side.

The title: *Where the Heart and Soul Reside.*

■ ■ ■

Sam

"What are you reading to Daria?" Mom asks.

I had paused, sensing her lurking in the doorway, listening. Curiosity has her coming in.

"A new Sonsy Falstaff novel soon to be released."

"Really?" Mom replies with equal amounts of excitement and surprise.

Mom is also a fan. In fact, it was her copy of another Falstaff novel that I first swiped, getting hooked, passing it on to others who thought to laugh at me for reading a romance novel. A put-up-or-shut-up moment. Vindicated. They started by reading a few passages. The juicy bits, the parts with passion and sex, got their attention; the quality writing had them delving deeper. Simple discussions in passing led to the Biker's Book Club we have today.

She reaches out in a silent command to let her see; I obey, placing the novel in her hand.

"*Where the Heart and Soul Reside.* Interesting title. Where did you manage to get a prereleased copy?"

"Found a stack of them in Daria's office. She's got several copies of each novel published by the author. This one too."

"Hmm. She must like the author's work too. Do you think she and the author know each other? Are friends? I heard Daria worked for a publishing house in New York, still does in some capacity. The more I know Daria, the more I like her. She's so faceted. Has depth."

"Read the inscription on the first page, Mom."

As she flips to that spot, I watch as Mom reads, then rereads. Reads it yet a third time before seeking my glistening eyes. Even now, I can't hide my tears.

"It's her? Daria. Daria is the author?" Mom whispers, clearing her throat. "What she writes here, about you..." Deep sigh. "Simply beautiful."

"Mom, has Mrs. Roth been here? Has she come to see her daughter after the crash?"

Mom nods. Relief has me hastily sitting. Instantly, Mom is at my side, pulling me into her side. Lovingly, she strokes my head, my back, soothing me the way she knows best.

"Tell me," I request.

"Seems Rachel is a bit of a sneak herself. Tiptoed in multiple times, when you were here asleep. Stayed nearly the entire time you were away. I was just speaking with her before I entered."

"I don't understand..."

"She's a proud woman who feels she is to blame for it all. Seems Daria inherited from Rachel low self-esteem, a lack of knowing one's self-worth, doubting it to the point where it becomes a self-fulfilling prophecy of a sort. Through your efforts, she is coming around, though at a turtle's pace. Until…seeing her child like this…" she says, gesturing to where Daria lies, silent save for the beeps of the machines, "Knowing she could have died…could still die." Pressing her hands to her breast, she says, "One of the worst things for a mother who truly loves her children."

What can I do but pull Mom into my arms? So entwined, mother and son rock each other, gaining comfort from one another and the knowledge that we truly are family that love each other, even when we blunder out of our sense of love.

Rachel Roth has blundered big time. Now she sees the light. Will she clearly emerge, becoming the mother she always sought to be? Love Daria, warts and all? Accept Daria for the wonderful person Daria is, regardless of who and what has made her unique?

Chapter 18

Daria

My walk around the block lasted well over a month. Seems that I took my time waking up, with the brain swelling and all. A month of my life, gone. Time I won't get back. Time with Sam and my babies stolen. A month without blogging, without observing the advent of spring, without working in the yard.

A month sleeping in Sam's arms while in a hospital bed. Though my brain can't recall it, my heart does.

Actually, nobody could get Sam to leave my side. I learned from one of my attending nurses that Sam stayed with me every night, first sleeping in the easy chair in the room. Later, he snuggled in bed alongside me. That only began when the doctors said that there was nothing more they could do but wait.

Coma. The doctor told me.

"I thought I was just dreaming. Everything was so peaceful. Soon it was too lonely. I've been alone for so long, and then along came Sam. Sam, you are my drug, my addiction. Gotta have it. Need my dose of Sam."

He places my palm over his lips, pressing a kiss there in the center before bringing our combined hands to his cheek. I feel his tears wetting my flesh.

"The delicious aroma that is you started flooding in. First it was faint, then kept getting stronger..."

"I placed one of my shirts over you, tucking another in and around your neck when I couldn't be here to hold you. Even brought in a sheet and pillow from home..."

"Yes," I say on an exhale. "It was your scent, your flavor that I sensed. I wanted it. *Needed* it. Craved it. It brought me back to the light. To you." I delight in how he continues playing with my fingers and hand.

"Tell me you didn't spend an entire month, day and night, here, Sam..."

"He wanted to," Mom says. "Between me, your father, Bunny, and Robert, we made him leave for a portion of the day. He has his company to run, two homes to look after, plus your pets. He wouldn't leave unless there were two of us in here with you at all times."

Mom comes to the side of my bed, gently tucking a strand of hair behind my ear. Bending toward me, she kisses my brow. Tears, genuine tears, are in her eyes.

"My darling daughter. I thought we...I...may have lost you." Her breath hitches. "That hit me hard." Eyes closing, squeezing them tightly shut, she breathes in a ragged breath.

"Mom? Mom."

A shake of her head. "No. Let me finish. I know I've hurt you. I've been so self-centered. So jealous. Angry at myself..."

"Why?" I'm truly bewildered.

"For being a failure. Failing you as a mother..."

"What? How do you figure that?"

"I had you when I was still craving that corporate life. I didn't really want to be tied down at home. That's what was expected. I didn't want to conform. When it was apparent you inherited the chubby gene that plagues the family…I saw how my aunts and others similarly afflicted were cruelly treated. I didn't want that for you. Didn't realize I was doing to you myself the very thing I feared others would. I became the tormentor I sought to save you from."

"Mom, you could have sent me to daycare. Instead you gave me to Aunt Alphia. That one move saved me. It was the best thing…"

"I was jealous," she admits. "You thrived under her care. When I came to collect you each afternoon, I saw how reluctant you were to leave her. Knowing that you liked her more than me…I'm ashamed of how I've acted toward you, the words I've said. What I've done." Silently, she weeps. "Asking for your forgiveness…" She shakes her head. "How can I when I'll never forgive myself?"

"Mom, there is no manual on how to love. I know you love me, have always loved me. There has always been that inside, no matter what you've said and done. But I can't…won't accept that anymore."

"We can start fresh," she says with hope written across her face and in each breath of her words.

"I'd like that. This time, can you just accept me? All of me? Each pound of me?"

"Done."

■ ■ ■

"Tom and Braden have been by a few times. You were still in a coma or resting. They've been worried, as brothers tend to be," Mom tells me as she's brushing my hair. It's something I find soothing. A mother-daughter bonding moment I relish.

"What about Victoria?"

Mom pauses ever so slightly. It's enough to have me noticing.

"Mom. I thought we agreed, no more secrets or avoidance of full disclosure."

There have been a few times since our breakthrough moment that I've had to remind Mom about the terms and conditions of this relationship. She's trying. I love her all the more for it.

"Hmm, your face looks thinner, Daria. I do believe you've lost weight."

"Outside of the month in the hospital, it's called sexercise, Mom. With Sam, I've indulged in lots and lots of it." Yeah, and the daily walks with Holly and Mistletoe have helped on that score. Our bond is still strong. Seems Sam brought them in disguised as service pets. Mistletoe has settled in the crook of my neck, purring up a storm while Holly snuggles over my legs.

Mom's blush is all that tells me she's heard.

"Mom. Back to Victoria…"

"She'll come round when it's right for her. She's got to work through her own feelings at her own speed. Just give her time. I fear she's too much like me. Jealous."

"Jealous? Of what?"

"Your heart. Talent. You brought in the better grades. Got all the personality compliments. Always the teacher's favorite. Hopping up and doing any chores needing doing. Giving up your life and career to look after Alphia…Good fortune always seems to follow you, no matter the obstacles tossed in your way. Victoria… Victoria chose to pick at those things that made her different from you. Better in her mind. Particularly those things that were praised and prized by society as a whole. Went out of her way to show how different and better she was."

"Weight."

Mom nods. "Always a touchy subject. A sore spot she could use and exploit. It was the only means she had to measure herself against you and in her mind not be found wanting. The one way to find and establish her worth."

"Worth." Scoffing. "Why does weight have to be the measure of how one is valued? My weight should be no more than a number. Recognized no more than the color of my hair or eyes or the color of my skin. It's simply a part of me. A product of my ancestry, lifestyle, and the environment in which I live. Weight is not all there is to know and learn of me. It doesn't define what and who I am as an individual."

"I've had my own epiphany on that score, daughter. Society says differently."

"Just who is this *society*? All give lip service to how wrong those opinions are, but none seek to directly challenge and change forever what we say is wrong." I scoff with a shake of my head until Mom places a hand on my crown to keep me from moving. "And you wonder why people become recluses? Hollandaise, I don't get such judgment from Holly or Mistletoe, and never from Sam. They love me unconditionally, warts and all. Society should start thinking and acting for themselves for a change, or keep their noses out of other people's business. Hey, news flash. Want to end-isms we say are bad, harmful, and not in the spirit of being an upstanding human being? Don't indulge in them."

Chapter 19

Daria

"What?" I ask in a half-chiding, half-defensive voice.

"Just you," Sam replies, snaking out his hand to touch me, any part of me.

Okay, so I look like a dog eager for a ride in the car. Who wouldn't? I've just been sprung from the hospital, and I'm on my way home. Home. My lap is full. Sam brought along Holly and Mistletoe. They are now both snuggled on me.

"Just so you know, once this ass gets inside, I'm never leaving."

"Daria."

I know that tone and what he's really saying.

"Okay, so what if I'm lying—sort of."

"We'll start out together, as a family, all four of us. Then go from there. Baby steps before the great leap, or your first solo. Besides, with the amount of work that's been building up since…while you were playing the role of Sleeping Beauty—and creepily beautifully, too, I might add—you'll probably want the break."

Hmmm. Grumpy me huffs, knowing he may be right. Sam did bring in a laptop, so I was able to get some work done. Went through emails. Read tons of blog comments. Responded to a few. Conducted a bit of research on what I plan to try next.

Sam and I had our first fight when I discovered that he'd been paying my bills as they came in. He thought accessing my online banking account was too personal, a violation of privacy codes. The man has been in every orifice on my body, has touched, licked, or kissed every inch of me and places within. And he thinks I'd mind him paying my bills by accessing my online account? Guacamole, I love this man.

"I told all in the neighborhood to stay away for a few days, give you a chance to gain your sea—or home—legs again. So it shouldn't be Grand Central Station for a while."

"Sam? Why do I hear a 'but'?"

"Well, you know the monthly block bashes?"

Holly whines.

"What she said. Tell me, Sam."

"I sort of agreed for us to host this time around."

Sam flinches when I narrow my eyes at him dangerously. Would have growled, too, but I thought it might scare the girls. I can already feel that Mistletoe needs a pedicure.

Snuggling with Mistletoe, I ask her in a baby voice, "What do you say to Daddy about what he's gone and done?" Her yap of a meow is the answer. Not to be outdone, Holly adds her two cents, echoing her sister's displeasure.

Sam ducks his head. He's worried. Well, he should be. Depending on what else I discover—he should be petrified.

"Who's expected to come? Because if Miss Thang, Bronco babe, the platinum blonde, thinks she is—"

"No!" Furious head shaking matches Sam's furiously spoken word. "I forgot to tell you. Bronco bitch no longer lives in the neighborhood." Happy bark from Holly. Say what? "Feeling she couldn't live down the incident and would always be known by her deed or the monikers awarded her, she put her house up for sale at a price meant to cement a swift closing."

"She's gone?" The need to verify is strong, fueling the desperate hope coloring my words.

"Uhm-hmm."

"What else? Loosen the lips and just spit it out, Pieman."

"Well, though you, the girls, and I are happy, others are…Not all are."

"Come again?"

"Daria, the lady was friends with others in the neighborhood. Close friends…"

Holding up a hand. "No. Don't tell me. Let me guess. Umm, Clarise and Tabitha."

Salami, olives, bacon, and tomato sandwich. I know it took a crackerjack attorney from Robert Bixby's firm to convince the Bronco bitch to cooperate and for her insurance to pay out for damages incurred on me due to her recklessness.

"What about the kid?"

"Nicholas?" I nod. "Seems the hooligan has woken up a bit and found a person, a young man, within, one with heart. At least one who now thinks and strives to live a life based on principles, not adolescent desire."

"Huh?"

"He's grown up a bit since then. Promising. Among other things, he has been filling his nonschool time with community service. On his own accord, he came by when I wasn't home. Seeing him, Mable suggested that he help with what you could not do, prepare the garden for spring. He fetches the eggs each day. Has raked up the leaves and debris you use as natural mulch, placing such in your compost bin. Cut back the brown so the green can come through. Mowed and hoed. Planted. Irene even comes down to give suggestions and supervise. Cyrus James as well. Seems Nicholas likes working the land, and Cyrus is thrilled to teach the kid the art of farming."

That has me startling. So much so that I have to keep both hands on the girls, who think something is going on. "Mean Irene, the one who thinks brown is the new green? A modern suburban, video-playing, music-blaring-through-earphones, cell phone addict of a kid is learning the art of farming?" What alternate strand in the universe did I awaken in?

"Actually, Daria, Irene isn't all that bad. In fact, I think you'd rather like her. Outside of differing views about watering, she knows how to tend a garden. Seems to know what plants you like and where. Seemed to know by the layout of the garden plots." He shrugs his shoulders.

Yeah, I bet. "Meaning she's been snooping…"

"Certainly. With her help and Cyrus James's, along with Nicholas's muscle, they've got things looking pretty nice. The grass is green, flowers blooming. Leaves are out in full. Seeds planted and beds marked. Other tender plants in the ground. What better time to celebrate life and your return home?"

"Hmmm. We'll see."

■ ■ ■

Once Sam pulls up into the garage, all thoughts about a block bash to be hosted here go out the window. I'm more interested in being home.

Holly and Mistletoe are happy to be home too. They shoot through the door to rediscover the space. Though a part of me wants to join the girls in their frolicking play and joy, when Sam opens the door leading from the garage, all I do is inhale.

"Awww. The scent of home." I open my eyes. "You know, there once was a time this was my favorite scent. Still tops the list, but now it's number two. Used to be the only thing outside of food that once upon a time could soothe me. No longer." I enter and calmly walk around my kitchen, caressing my appliances as if they are long-lost family and friends.

Sam tilts his head. "If it's no longer this place, your sanctuary, what is it, babe?" Setting down my bag of hospital belongings in the utility room, he follows me. His eyes never leave me, gleaming with some inner light.

Walking up to him as bold as I've ever been, I press full-bodily against my lover. Closing my eyes, once again, I inhale, running my nose around his form, sniffing him from head to…head. "You."

Sam's hands are on my shoulders. He pulls me farther in as his face descends, locking lips on mine. Coming up for air. "Take me to bed."

■ ■ ■

"Too much?" Sam's husky voice penetrates the sex haze that coats my brain. He punctuates his words with a snap of his hips, pushing Frank B. Swellington deeper home.

First a shake of my head. Gasps, then gasping out a reply. "No. Never too much. Never enough. Always more."

Sam presses his forehead against mine. "It's the same with me. We shall always remain this way. Bodies entwined. Hearts tethered by that invisible twine of love. Forever bound. Souls merged into an eternal one…"

"Sam, you're a poet." I exhale a staccato breath when he moves his hips so, gasping as a rush of delight attempts to overwhelm me.

With a quick kiss on the tip of my nose, Sam says, with a

degree of smugness, "Uh-uh. A plagiarist. Stolen words from a stolen novel."

"What, my man, a word thief?" Silence is his response. Shifting my pelvis, I ask, "Sam?" I know the source of those words. They're mine. I just want to hear it from him. Coitus seems to be a truth serum of sorts with my Sam.

"Babe. Gotta tell ya. When I was in your office…"

"Find a surprise?" Man, gotta help the guy out. "It was meant to be a birthday present for you, one that included your bookish biker brothers."

"What you wrote…the gift…the revelation…Do you know how proud I was, and am, will always be of you? Never, ever, ever, *ever* write yourself off again. Look what you've managed to accomplish when you were hidden from the world, from life…"

"Sam."

"No, babe. You listen to me. Rapture doesn't come close to what I felt. Still feel. All the emotions that ever were and will be and then some that have no words, but a knowing. Think of what you can accomplish when you fully reenter the world."

"Really? Like what?"

"Dream it, and you can do and be it. See it done successfully so," he tells me between thrusts.

Lying back in the pillows of our bed, I savor his attention, his moves and motions. Realization hits as I come, he comes, we come together.

"I no longer need to dream, Sam. Reality is my dream. Each step taken, each day with you, is a dream come true."

Chapter 20

Daria

Stars sparkle before my eyes like silver sugar-ball sprinkles do on wedding cakes. I've been sampling them a bit too much of late. It's one part of my upcoming wedding that I've decided to have another professional create.

These stars that swirl before my face, obscuring my vision, are no confectioner's creation. In fact, I feel as if I have sunk into a new depth of neighborhood hell.

"Oh my God!" Mable gasps. In her next breath, she is ordering someone to go fetch Sam.

"Daria, lay still. Don't move."

Groaning my acquiescence, I remain where I lie, pancaked on top of the collapsed lawn chair Clarise had earlier ushered me into.

Apple fritters, I should have not allowed myself to be enticed by her sugar substitute sweetness. Fake. Still deadly. Lulled by the recent transformation of my relationship with my Mom. That's what it was. Too hopeful that the world had truly changed along with her. As my senses come back online, my nose picks up a different fragrance, and not of that fried pippin, cinnamon, and sugary bits of goodness. The aroma is coming from what pillows my head and is now oozing about my ears.

Shit.

Dog shit, to be precise.

Added to that realization is the irritating twittering of the two demented neighborhood birds identified as Clarise and Tabitha. Both stand there. Laughing. Laughing at me.

I furrow my brow when I hear, sotto voce, "Did I do it right, Aunt Clarise? I did exactly what you said to do."

"Shh. Go get another cookie. They're your favorite. Take two or more if you like." Eager child's steps move away as the ladies continue to giggle and laugh at my expense.

At first, I find myself retreating in the fashion that I had vowed to leave in my past. It appears all transformations, be they parental relationships or personal growth, have their fragile moments. There will be times that try one's soul, when things appear dark before the new day. When shit shouldn't be happening, but it does. It does. Double scoop of Holly logs. This is no single pile pillowing my head.

Desperately, I fight against closing my eyes. Shutting my vision to it all. Collapsing my hearing to the humiliating laughter it was meant to evoke. I fight against hiding from the mortification threatening to overwhelm me. Already its hot stain is heating my cheeks.

Oxygen is hard-pressed to return inside my winded lungs. My throat is so tightly squeezed only a trickle of a sob pushes to escape. Clamping down on that urge, I refuse to allow it to surface. Bring forth the fury. Let righteous rage emerge. She will gladly do battle this day.

Instead, the sweet ick of dog poop is slightly abated by the familiar comforting scent of my Sam.

Breathless. "Daria!" He collapses at my side. "Don't be so quick to move." He presses me back easily when I wiggle-struggle to rise to a sitting position. He is not alone. His pack of biker brothers and their ladies, my friends, have gathered around.

"I shouldn't have left you alone," Sam self-reproaches.

That gets a growl from me.

"Can you speak?" Wheezing is my response. "Ah, got the wind knocked out of you. Anything hurt besides pride?" How well my man knows me.

Lamely gesturing.

"Your ass?" He chuckles. "I promise to kiss all of it and make it better."

A calculating sparkle enters my eye. Followed by a wicked gleam.

"Don't let this slide you back," he whispers close to my ear before pulling back. Yeah, get a whiff of that? Uhm-hmm.

"Lo…looks…like I've…land…landed in another pile…of shit," I manage to choke out.

A pair of designer deck shoes appears in my prone peripheral vision. "Hey, Sam. Don't know why that chair was brought over and set out. Clarise's nephew must have lugged it over. Been meaning to toss it. It's broken. Daria didn't bust it."

"Come again?" Sam and I question together, his voice firm, mine a bit thready.

All twittering laughter coming from Clarise and Tabitha suddenly ceases. The glaring crowd rounding on them gives me cover as Sam and a few others help pull me up into a sitting position. The shifting weight of the move causes the last vestiges of the aluminum and canvas frame of the chair to further collapse. The sudden jolt triggers globs of poop crumble to fall from my head and hair, where more clings.

"Take your time," Sam speaks softly. Placing a supportive hand on my shoulder, he rises to his feet, assuming his full height and then some, or so it seems from my angle.

"Morris, you telling me this was a setup? Done deliberately to Daria? A human being, and one recently home from over a month's stay in hospital while healing from head trauma?" My man advances. "This was all designed to make her look like she was responsible for breaking an already broken chair and land, headfirst, smack in a pile of calculatedly placed shit?" Menacing growls chorus around from friends and neighbors.

"Not his fault, Sam," I remind him, tugging on his pants leg as I wobble like a Weeble still seeking to gain its balance, both emotional and physical.

"No, but it's hers," rings out a voice back from the grave of sisterhood. Victoria. Hot on her heels? Mom. Both filled with righteous anger. Double Furies ablaze with fire. Huh?

Like an avenging Valkyrie, Victoria descends on the two females. "This is your doing? Finding jollies by setting others up? Rising on the back of those you push into the dirt and shit? Did you give a thought about your victim? She's just out of the hospital. Your neighbor. A human being. Does none of that register? Matter?" Victoria advances toward the two retreating women, who are tossing supplicating glances at their men, seeking their assistance and aid in extracting them from the spiraling scene.

Victoria continues to bring it. The two ladies seem to be left to stew in their own mess. No help is coming. As friends and Mom focus on helping me, I turn eager eyes on my sister.

"What sick reason did you have for deliberately placing Daria in that chair, knowing it would break? Placing poop strategically so?"

"It was a joke," Tabitha retorts, flicking the length of her jaunty ponytail over her shoulder, trying to turn her back on Victoria.

As fast and as unexpected as a lightning strike, Victoria slaps Tabitha across the cheek. "Got a problem with that? Is that a joke?" Victoria barks to the stunned woman, who now holds her throbbing, reddened cheek. The other cheek is starting to flame. Its source is another heat—humiliation. Tabitha turns her back, cowed, weeping.

There is still another foe to vanquish.

"Payback," Clarise seethes, stepping up to the challenge. She won't be as easily dismissed or routed as Tabitha.

"For being kind and generous? For Daria's talent in her garden, as well as in the kitchen? Then there is her successful blog and her published novels." Turning to me, she says, "Daria, you should so write about this in your next book."

Clarise's face begins to pale.

Rounding on Clarise, Victoria is only getting started. More desperate glances toward Clarise's yet unmoved husband speak volumes. Humiliation and understanding are doing a color number on Clarise's face and her visible facial expressions and body language. That alone speaks volumes.

Me? By this time, I've been helped to my feet, generally assessed by Mom and Sam. I'm staying put, refusing any and all suggestions to retreat into one of our homes. Why leave in the middle of an epic showdown? Besides, my hair is filled with poop. My whispered words to such effect have Stephanie and Paige running inside to gather what is needed to clean me up, leaving me to watch Victoria take down Clarise.

A wall of women and male friends help to maintain my privacy as Paige and Mom help me peel off my shit-stained shirt, wetting and shampooing my hair with the hose.

"Eew," Paige exclaims. "It's even behind your ears."

"Well, get it off, then." My snarky tone has my personal bathers giggling and snapping into action. Three pairs of hands work independently yet cooperatively and with love to rid me of the recent filth. It is more than the dog shit that is washed away. In a sense, it is a new baptism of sorts.

Here I am standing outside, clad in only my bra and jeans, surrounded by people who love and like me. Each one is coming to my aid. Some washing my hair. Others standing guard, while others advance into battle as my champion. All are defending me. Me!

What Clarise and Tabitha intended was more than a prank gone wrong. The overall plan—simple. The execution—perfectly flawless. What was not expected is what resulted—ultimately their downfall. Hoisted by their own poop petard.

Clean hair encased in a turban-twisted towel; new, clean, loose-fitting blouse in place; anchored into Sam's side, I take in the last of the show, basking in being surrounded by friends and loved ones. People who value me, who have never written me off but in fact have been readers, fans, friends, family, and lover.

"Daria is a joke." Clarise scoffs, circling around as a trapped and cornered feral beast might. "Who would want...that?" She gestures to all of me.

"Me!" Sam exclaims. The forceful explosiveness of his pronouncement causes Clarise to take a retreating step.

"Me," Joe echoes his words, stepping forward.

"Me," Paige shouts out before others do the same.

Mable, Jim, Cyrus, Irene, the biker boys—with their new novels clutched in their hands and a few tucked into the back pockets of their jeans. My phalanx of friends and family. Even Nicholas steps forward.

Clarise stands alone. Even her husband has deserted her.

"God, can't anyone take a joke anymore?" Clarise laughs darkly, trying to gain some support from the watchful and silent crowd.

"Oh, sure. Everyone likes a jolly at someone else's folly." Victoria waltzes right up to Clarise, smashing a handful of poop right into Clarise's kisser. "Eat shit, you foulmouthed vermin. Don't you think this is funny?"

"Well-deserved." This coming from Mable, who begins the applause.

"And so is this." Flicking out her arm, Victoria wipes poop residue onto Tabitha's designer-label top. Clarise's sister in crime had not budged. Now the two are screaming through screwy faces, ewing and plehing to a strange dance that includes tongue spluttering and stomping in place and swishing hands over face and clothing. Their antics get laughs and guffaws from the crowd of onlookers. Finally unable to take any more, the two of them run.

That was the last I ever saw of them.

Chapter 21

Sam

"Now there's a woman, and a beast," Joe says, catching me and all by surprise.

Marching right up to Victoria, heedless of her shit-smeared hand, he yanks her into him, then proceeds to show her his appreciation and admiration by kissing her into dizziness.

Wolf whistles and applause break out while I hug my Daria tightly to my side. When Joe finally breaks his lip-lock on Victoria, he escorts her to Daria's side. Daria, in turn, enfolds her sister as their mother wraps her arms around both of her daughters.

"Victoria?" Longing fills her tone as Daria speaks her sister's name.

"No, Daria. Let me. It's me that needs to speak now." Shame has her turning away before resolve has her turning back. "I must apologize, need to, want to. Can you ever forgive me and resurrect me from the death-pile of stupid sisterhood gone too far?"

"Always. Instantly," croons my love, my lady.

"Just what are you apologizing for?" I say, inserting myself into the conversation. Twin blinking owls meet my words. "Hey, there will be no ambiguity here. Clear, concise, precise. That's the language we speak in this family, in this relationship." I'm putting my foot down for all to see. Daria may be the queen of my world, but I am king in this castle and will see to the safety of all within, shoring up battlements where needed.

Daria gives me that sideways smile I find adorable. Head gesturing to me, she says, "You heard the man…"

Victoria appears to be checking the workability of her jaw. She keeps opening and closing that maw of hers. Did Joe manage to damage her in that heady kiss? Furtive eyes flash to me.

"No running off to do this in private. Sincerity and the severity of the issue dictate that this must be done in the out and open. Nothing less will do," I pontificate, laying down the law.

"You were what I'd always longed to be, except…"

"Fat." Drolly spoken by Daria.

Victoria nods. "I used that as a weapon to hurt you. A way to lash out with my jealousy. Whenever I compared—"

"See, that was your first mistake," Daria interrupts. "You are not me. Never have been and never will be. Work on being yourself, the unique you, not some facsimile of someone else. Aunt Alphia, and now Sam, have helped me to understand and believe that I am one of a kind. I don't want any replicas of me. That lesson applies to you too. There is and will be only one Victoria Summer Roth. Be that person and no other."

Looking beyond Victoria, she says knowingly, "Joe, once Victoria cleans up a bit, will you be so kind as to escort my sister to the food so she can get herself a plate?"

Joe eagerly steps forward, a rare gleam in his eyes, extending a gentleman's elbow to the badass babe who singlehandedly vanquished the neighborhood demonic diva dictator and sidekick.

■ ■ ■

Two days later, guess whose homes went up for sale? Seems the neighborhood is bleeding bad blood. None are sad to see either of those women go. Heard tell that Clarise was served divorce papers in a shoebox. Well, if it fits...

Happier still is the knowledge that both homes are under contract to guys in my biker's club. I've fully moved into Daria's home, and Joe and his new lady have moved into my old home next door.

In the weeks that follow, more amazing transformations are in store. Daria has her sit-down heart-to-heart with Victoria. What comes out is a new, blooming relationship—not just between sisters but one between Joe and Victoria as well—and an announcement that Victoria wants to try her hand at operating a food truck. A food truck serving up dishes crafted by Daria. Daria agrees. *For the Love of Food* is going mobile.

Victoria, it seems, can be quite lovely when she's pounded down her horns. She's learning that flinging honey gets her more places than flinging manure, though it took that handful of poop for her to see just what a shit she'd been and the power that love can bring to those worthy of wielding its blade and exposing one's heart for the sake of another.

Joe and a team of guys are busy transforming a van to match Victoria's dream on wheels, cooked up by Daria and Victoria.

Things couldn't be busier. Daria still cooks, creates, blogs, and writes. All this she has managed to do while organizing our wedding. Of course, the once-invisible woman now has a host of helpers eager to lend a hand. We've selected the Saturday of Memorial Weekend to be our big day.

■ ■ ■

Thumb and forefinger inserted in mouth, I whistle to gain the attention of my groomsmen. Under my arm, I carry a box that

Daria insists contains the gift tradition dictates must be given by the groom to his mates.

"What's this?" Keevan asks.

"Presents. So says Daria." I shrug while peeling off the packing tape sealing the box shut.

"Holy crap," Foster exclaims, swatting away Joe's grabby hands as he attempts to reach in the box and extract what's there.

We're all stunned. Me the most. With hands that tremble, I smooth away the Bubble Wrap and tissue paper that hide the cover of Sonsy Falstaff's latest novel.

"Even when I think I've got her all figured out, she still manages to pull something like this..." I say, holding up a book for all to see.

"On the cover, is that...her?"

"Uh-huh." Daria on rare display, in a form only I have been privy to so far.

There, lying back across the cover for all to see, is the woman soon to be my wife. No longer does she hide, but she has exposed herself to the world, come what may. Her luscious hind hair is seductively strewn over the pillowy bed upon which she lays. The beguiling sexiness matches her pose, a three-quarter turn of her prone body. Head and face slightly turned as if looking at a lover. Lips painted a dark red, slightly parted with a shmear of white cream along the corner.

Naked.

An arm is lazily placed to shield most of her breasts yet reveal their alluring, round fullness. Nothing but silky and smooth, creamy, bare skin until reaching that triangular patch at the junction of her thighs and legs. There sits a perfectly sliced piece of mixed-berry pie.

The title of this master work? *The Zen of Eating Pie.*

I collapse into the nearest chair.

On the exact day she will openly declare her devotion and love to me, she declares the newfound love she has for herself. This was not just a gift to those who stand behind me, behind us, but a whopper of a gift to me.

My lady no longer hides. No longer is she invisible. Today our lives will be forever twined before all that is holy, before family and friends. Our new life is about to begin. A new chapter and new novel with endless possibilities. No longer are wadded-up dreams tossed in the wastebasket of life's despair. No longer written off.

EPILOGUE

Daria

Our wedding day was better than the one envisioned in my dreams. Each day since has been the same. I'm living my dream. Not saying it's perfect. No life ever is, but for, me what I have is my dream come true. My dream home. Dream career—not a job but work I have a passion for, so it never feels like work, though at times it can be hectic. A dream of a man whom I always seem to have a passion for, and he for me.

Go figure.

He did, and now so do I.

"Sam. Saaam." I whisper him awake on the morning of our first anniversary as a married couple. "Happy anniversary, husband."

He flutters his eyes open, stretches, then gives me his lazy and oh-so-sexy grin.

Reaching his hand to cup the back of my neck gently, he pulls me forward, giving me my morning kiss. Sam's kisses still have the ability to steal my breath away.

"Have I told you I love you today?" he huskily inquires.

"Not with words but in other ways," I sigh, my lips barely a breath away from his. I begin to worry when a frown creases his brow. Instantly, he rolls us, placing me underneath with him looming over me.

Looking deep into my eyes, he whispers, "That needs to be rectified immediately, Mrs. Bixby." One hand holds my cheek, keeping me still as his nose and lips course around my face and throat, punctuating places with kisses, nibbles, and licks. Tickling his lips near my ear. "I. Love. You."

In answer, I spread my legs as wide as my smile. "Perfect fit," I say when he slips Frank B. Swellington into my heated and moist oven.

Kisses and caresses quickly turn into prolonged morning nooky. Nothing stops us from our morning pleasure, save one. As we're in midthrust, an egg timer near the bed sounds. Its manic vibrating rattle sends it nearly toppling off the bedside table.

"What's that for? You baking something? Got something going in the oven?" Sam raises his head high above our joined bodies, sniffing for anything tantalizing that might be wafting from the kitchen. Curious glance down at my still and prone form. "Can't smell anything but your arousal's aroma, babe."

The gleam in his eye says it titillates him too. So does the nip on my neck. Leaning my head to the side gives him further access to that erogenous zone and gives me a chance to peek at the stick in the glass.

"Yeah," I reply, trying hard to swallow my happy tears and keep from bursting into joyful laughter. There is no hiding from Sam.

Again, he pauses. "What? Tell me, babe."

"Yeah, I got something baking. Baking in *my* oven."

"Need to go check so it doesn't burn? Need a test subject, 'cause, babe, you know I'm your man."

"How sweet," I praise. "No, thanks. I'm rather enjoying what we're cooking up right here, right now." His hand skimming over my flesh tells me he likes my words.

"Got to learn these new curves, babe. You've lost weight, less of your body to love on."

"I'm glad. But you know they will be changing again over the months to come, on account of what's baking." Oh yeah, it is becoming increasingly difficult to contain my laughter.

Passion and confusion cloud eyes that search out mine. "Babe?"

Groaning. "Can I keep going, or are we gonna have to run to the kitchen?"

"Keep going until bliss is achieved, please."

And he does.

Afterward, he nestles me into his side. Idly, he runs a hand up and down my back and butt. Suddenly, the hand stills.

Peering down at me, he asks, "Daria, just how long does this thing you're making need to bake? Is it a new recipe?"

"Well, not so new. But this one will be uniquely different, one of a kind. Been done forever, but I've not done it before. So this is new for me, a learning opportunity. One I'm counting on your help to make it come out juust right." I smile. "In answer to your question, all in all, it should take about seven months or so before the final product is done."

"Sev...Seven months? Did I hear that right? What are you baking?"

"Sam, I've got a bun in the oven. Made with our special batter mix. It'll take about seven months or so before it's fully ready to emerge."

Mom, BB, and others have warned me that men can be a bit dense at such a time. They weren't fooling. Reaching over Sam, who thought it a grand opportunity to nibble on one of my protruding, ultrasensitive nipples, I rummage in the drawer in search of what I planned on gifting Sam later this morning.

Finding it, I exclaim, "Here, you can read about it in my next novel."

Releasing my nipple, he takes hold of the book. "Another novel by my favorite author, Sonsy Falstaff. Title..."

"Title?" I urge.

"*You, Me, and Baby Makes Three.*"

The End

ABOUT THE AUTHOR

Catherine has lived a life filled with adventure. Her eclectic tastes come naturally along with an abundance of curiosity and the thirst to explore the world around her. Her life's experiences as a member of a military family often traveling and relocating to places around the world have helped with that. This semi-nomadic life helped foster a love of history, reading, and adventure, sparking her imagination. Further adventures were encouraged by her family as she matured, resulting in months and years spent in overseas education and travel. By the age of twenty-four, she had visited every continent but one. Years as a historical reenactor and interpreter fueled her drive to teach. For over twenty years Catherine was a high school history teacher before she began to seriously write down the stories filling her head. When not writing, Catherine can be found traveling with her husband, working in her garden or taking walks with Mr. Pickles.